陽光心語

WORD OF SOUL IN THE SUNSHINE

陽光 著

五洲传播出版社

图书在版编目（CIP）数据

阳光心语 ： 汉英对照 / 陽光著. -- 北京 ： 五洲传播出版社, 2019.3

ISBN 978-7-5085-4107-5

Ⅰ. ①阳… Ⅱ. ①阳… Ⅲ. ①随笔一作品集一中国一当代一汉、英 Ⅳ. ①I267.1

中国版本图书馆CIP数据核字(2019)第030785号

陽光心語

著　　者：陽　光
译　　者：王民卉
出 版 人：荆孝敏
责任编辑：樊程旭
装帧设计：曹　乐
出版发行：五洲传播出版社
地　　址：北京市海淀区北三环中路31号生产力大楼B座6层
邮　　编：100088
发行电话：010-82005927，010-82007837
网　　址：http://www.cicc.org.cn，http://www.thatsbooks.com
印　　刷：河北文盛印刷有限公司
版　　次：2022年3月第1版第1次印刷
开　　本：16开
印　　张：20
字　　数：150千字
定　　价：78.00元

■ 目 录/Contents

不足为“序”

方 宁

我们正处在一个“心灵鸡汤”四溢、自媒体火爆的大众娱乐时代，应该说最不缺少的就是文字的盛宴了。而微信的出现，更时时撩拨着人们的创造欲并制造着普遍化阅读的机会。南宋词人叶梦得尝言：“凡有井水处，即能歌柳词”，是说柳永词的阅读无障碍，故普及化程度高。而环视今日，凡有人聚处，皆为手机痴。此种情景，亦为天下之奇观也。

的确，当今国人的阅读呈现着深刻的矛盾，一方面是严重的匮乏，据统计，普通人对纸媒书刊的年阅读量处于历史的最低水平；另一方面又是极度的繁荣，人们通过手机微信及各种电子媒介所进行的阅读活动，无所不包，无处不在，尤其是自媒体流行以来，聪明的国人随时可以开启从写作到发表的模式，而浏览那些泛滥于网络的文字和图像，遂成大众围观者津津乐道之事。难怪有人戏称：而今还有什么比发表自己的文字更容易的事情吗！

事实上，当“写作”成为大众传播时代最没有难度的行为时，进入我们眼帘的每一行字、每一幅图，都有可能使我们成为别人所娱乐的对象，尤其是那些文字穿着貌似清新、时尚外衣的时候。

也许是因为职业的关系，经常与传统纸媒和文字图像打交道，我会格外注意娱乐化时代的种种文化奇观与人们的表演，看着那些颇具才情的写手，辗转腾挪，口吐莲花，或改写历史，或扭曲经典。当然，此中既有善做“心灵鸡汤”的大师，也有精于指鹿为马的“智者”，总之，十八般武艺尽出，足以令观者眼花缭乱。

但是在我看来，当善行与善意也能成为招摇过市的旗帜，其实并无异于恶行与恶意所带来的灾难。在我所见到的大量以文字图像构筑的王国里，似乎每一人都能成为上帝的使者、尧舜的代言，而遗憾的是，众多的写作者往往热衷于在文字表演的光鲜之上用力，而并未将目光落在价值实践的层面。

我的年轻同事陽光，或许让我的上述判断多少显得有些杞人忧天，甚至，或许他让我改变了对当今世界的某种程度的悲观。一个多月前，他先是将自己的美术作品集配以精美的文字送来，并嘱我为“序”，才知道在自己的身边，竟然还蛰伏着这样一位充满才情与创造力的青年。我所知道的是，慧峰常常以“陽光”为名参与各种公益活动，自然在这本书里，便时时呈现着清澈与温润的暖意。虽然他的文字，如果细细咀嚼，仍然可以感觉出“心灵鸡汤”的俗趣，但他却是一个肯于从自己的价值观出发的热情而坚定的实践者。不仅是眼前的这些用心与文字所编织的世界，他更重要的，却是少说而多做的善行。

在越来越喧嚣的世界中，他的“心语”宛如一道清流，自在山间低徊。还有什么比这种生命的形式更富于“阳光”的意味呢！

方宁

（作序者为中国艺术研究院编审，原《文艺研究》杂志社社长、主编）

Preface

FANG Ning

Editor, Chinese Art Research Institution;

Head and Chief Editor, Art Research Publishing House.

(This really is not qualified for a preface, but here it goes.)

We are in the era of popular entertainment full of so-called "chicken soup for the soul" or encouraging and inspirational words, as well as ebullient self-media, so it should be said that what is not missing is the feast of words. The emergence of WeChat, moreover constantly stimulates people's desire to write and to provides reading opportunities for all. In the Southern Song Dynasty, Ye Mengde said, "Wherever there is a well for water, there are people reciting Liu Yong's poems." It is said that no difficulties existed for people to read Liu Yong's poems, which is to say his poems were highly popular. Around the world today, everywhere people gather, there are those who are addicted to smart phones. This phenomenon can be a "wonder of the world" in itself.

Indeed, there is a profound contradiction regarding Chinese people's reading habits today. On the one hand, there exists a serious shortage. According to statistics, the annual reading amount of print material by ordinary people is at the lowest level in history. On the other hand, reading market is extremely prosperous, and people's reading activities through WeChat and various electronic media are seen everywhere. Since the appearance of the popular self-media, smart people can use any publishing template to write and publish. Browsing the over-flowing words and images on the Internet also becomes a popular public pastime. No wonder people joke that there is nothing easier nowadays than publishing one's own words!

In fact, when writing becomes an activity that requires no difficulty during the age of mass communication, every line of words we read and every picture we see, can make us the object of other people's creation for entertainment, especially when the words and pictures are covered under a seemingly pure, fresh, and noble cloak. Perhaps because of my professional background dealing with the traditional printing media, texts and images, I pay special attention to all kinds of cultural phenomenon and people's behavior in today's world of entertainment, while looking at those talented writers with their flowery language rewriting history or distorting the classics. Of course, there are masters of "chicken soup for the soul" and "wise men" who are good at "calling a stag a horse". On such a stage, 18 kinds of martial arts are enough to dazzle the audience.

But in my opinion, when benevolence and kindness are used as the banners by the swaggers in the streets, they are no less than the disaster caused by vice and malice. In many publications I have seen that are built on words and images, it seems that everyone can be the envoy of God and the publicist of Yao and Shun. But unfortunately, many writers tend to be keen on the superficiality in order to show off and do not focus on the true practical value of their work.

My young colleague, Yang Guang, has made my judgment somewhat groundless fears, or perhaps he made me change my pessimism about the world today. More than a month ago, he sent to me his art collection with fine writing and asked me to write a preface. Not until then did I know that a young man full of intelligence and creativity is right on my side. His pen-name is the same as the word "sunshine", and in this book, the writing is always clear and warm. Although his words, if read carefully, can still render the feeling of "chicken soup for the soul", he himself is a passionate and firm practitioner who is willing to carry out his own values. He creates the world with both the heart and the words, but more importantly, he does more good deeds than his words.

In an increasingly noisy world, his "language from the heart" is like a cool spring, meandering in the mountain. What could be more "sunshine" than this form of lifestyle!

第一章

人生感悟篇 / Inspiration in Life

不怕你有欲望，就怕欲望来临时难以自控。

心量大的人之所以快乐，不是因为他拥有的多，而是因为他计较的少。

乘坐高铁坐过站，好比一个人脱离了人生目标，如果继续前行就会离目标越来越远，唯有回头才是正道。

舞台大小决定着观众的多少，平台大小决定你能力的强弱。没有观众捧场，你唯有退场；有能力没平台，注定会失败或默默无闻。

对于那些懂得感恩和传递大爱的人，祖上积累的阴德和福报不但用不完，还会添福。而对于那些只知道贪图享受、不懂因果、不做善事的人，等把祖上的福报消受完，便会一无所有。

总认为自己很完美的人，容易在自我陶醉中丢失自我。

人生的经历写在脸上，人生的故事湮没在历史里。

人生短暂，转瞬即逝。缘去缘留，唯有缘分难求。

无论顺缘、逆缘，你都要惜缘、随缘，不要攀缘。因为，所有的缘都在你那一念之间。

随缘是智慧，随便即愚蠢。

随缘做事，能让人遇事冷静，从容对境。随便做人，则会让自己违缘不断，甚至招致麻烦和祸患。

人生最大的收获不是一个人走向成功，而是有一个懂你的人陪着你历经风雨、静观彩虹，相知到老。

人的幸福感不是源于你拥有多少地位和财富，而是取自你内心的丰富和满足。

不要因外表不及他人而心生烦恼，讨厌自己的身体。相由心生，容貌可以因修养而改观，气质可以因境界得到提升。

人生有太多的愿与不愿、要与不要、爱与不爱。

与其矛盾挣扎，不如以一颗平静的心，去接纳我们所不能改变的事物，去改变那些有可能改变

的东西，发现我们内心世界中可以突破的地方去突破，在不可突破的地方学会接纳。

这样，你的生活就会多些快乐，少些烦恼，多些甜蜜，少些苦涩。

世间本无痛苦，只是你还没有学会放下，握得越紧越无法自拔。

时过境迁，过后再回头看才发现那都不算什么。

人生存所需的物质其实很有限，而人的欲望无边。

如果过分追求物质享乐，就会变成欲望的奴隶。

治理雾霾不仅是政府和环保部门的事，而且是每一个公民应尽的责任。

如果每个人都能自觉行动起来爱护环境，爱护地球，雾霾就会不治而退。

如果你发现了他人之小过，先要反躬自身相同的问题，然后包容而隐忍；如果你发现了他人之大过，先要对照自鉴，还要用通达的道理、真诚的态度及时告诫对方改其过。

比你年龄大但德行不好的人，你要敬而远之；比你年龄小且德行好的人，你要诚心敬重。

一个人培养自己福田最好的方法不是烧香磕

头，而是无论物质生活条件怎么变化，你都能坚持最初的生活节俭，不过度浪费。

你心生贪、嗔、痴时，别人能看出来。而你心生嫉妒和傲慢时，不仅别人看不出来，连你自己也未必能及时察觉得到。

身体所受之苦是一时的，心灵所受之苦是一世的。

要想不让心受苦，就要改变自身贪、嗔、痴、慢、疑的习气。

当你被黑暗包围时，不要一味抱怨人心的失落和愤慨，请先挖掘自己内心的阳光，用心底的善念向周围展示慈悲的光芒。

在大爱者的眼里，每个人都是珍贵的，且是独一无二的，都有善良和大爱的潜能与本质，平等无分别。

如果被欲望控制，人就成了欲望的奴隶。如果控制了欲望，人就成为生命的主人。

不要在自己的世界里无限制地追求物质方面的享受。

当你的贪图享尽时，那没有被物质满足的灵魂将被折磨得体无完肤。

不要丢失原本的快乐，盲目追寻更大幸福。其实内心丰盈才是人生最圆满真实的富有。

生活中过于追逐利益的人很多，但大富大贵者却很少。

低调而谦和，喜欢把功劳拱手相让的人，名望反而会很高。

贫穷之因不只是懒惰，还有吝啬与自私。

富有者，必然要心胸广阔，怀摄天下。

当你真心做事利他而不为己，富贵才会青睐你！

在这个世界上，能够给予你健康、平安、快乐的不是别人，而是你自己与生俱来的那颗智慧、善良的本心。

如果说被人信任是一种幸福，同理，信任别人也会给自己增添幸福的机会。

生性多疑的人很难交到真朋友。

做一件好事容易，做一辈子好事难。

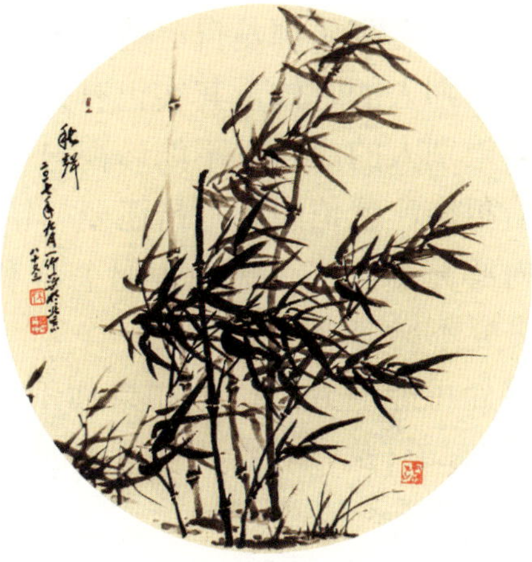

如果你每天做的事儿都能有利于别人，那做一辈子好事自然就不难了。

快乐不是别人给予的，而是自己争取的。

因为，你快不快乐只有自己心里最清楚。

生活中，没有人理所应当地帮你。

在你需要帮助时，无论别人是否帮上你的忙都要心存感激。

千万不能因没得到帮助，便对其心存怨恨。

生病时要放宽放平心态。

从容对一切人、一切事、一切物，绝不要用虚妄之心，你的身体也会随心境的变化好转。正所谓：事从容则有余味，人从容则有余年。

永远不要认为自己所遇到的痛苦都是别人的错，其实一切喜怒哀乐都是自己造成的。

你在仰望别人的时候，其实也有人在仰望你。

与其仰望别人的成功，不如珍视自己的现在。

人不怕犯错，就怕明知是错还要一错再错。

只要内心充满阳光，无论岁月怎样移驰，你的那颗童心终究不会变老。

生活随处可能遇到障碍，如果你不能客观地省察自身的问题，只是一味怨天尤人，最后的结局一定比想象中的严重。

如果别人诽谤你的声誉，请先审视自身的原因，一定是你在某些事情上给了对方诽谤的机会。

电影、电视剧里的剧情多是虚实结合的故事而已，千万不要过分投入而迷失自己。切勿盲目追随模仿，伤人误己！

一个人内心清净时看别人身上都是优点，反之，自己有什么缺点，就会看到别人身上类似的不足。

从我们身边看到或得到的权力、财富其实都不是真正的福报，真正的福报是无论缘来缘去，自己都不受影响，精神依然自在富足。

人一生中总会遇到很多问题，但不一定所有问题都有答案。

其实，与其执着答案，不如告诉自己平安快乐要比知道答案更重要。

上帝给予了你美丽的容颜，你带给了世人美的享受。

上帝赐予你博爱的心，你把爱化作阳光普照大地。

你的美和你的爱，将留在人间与天地共存。

不常写字的人，若送一把扇子叫他写，他越想写好，结果可能还不及平常效果。

这是因为预期成功、忧虑过甚的缘故。

事实上，对于成功预期过甚者，往往反而不能成功。对失败忧虑过甚者，往往反致失败。

当一些“热点新闻”在网上恶意炒作时，请你理性思考，别盲目跟贴四处转发。

其实，这些伎俩只是某些人获取利益的一种手段。

无论大喜还是大悲亲临你的生活，都要保持冷静。

此时，如果不能很好地管理自己的情绪，那你将会变成情绪的奴隶。

吃素的好处和意义与追求时尚、个人信仰毫无关联。

当你身心真正参与其中时，才发现自己吃的是一种绿色和谐、安全可靠的饮食文化。

解决心结和仇恨，最好的办法并不是执着和报复，而是给心换个环境，靠时间去氧化那些无名。

你所做的一切不可能让每个人都满意，所以不要为了讨好别人而丢失自己的本性，因为欣赏你的人永远都在支持你！

不要在生病后，才反思平时没好好爱惜自己的身体。

在别人生病时，你的一个微笑、一句问候足以支撑起对方早日康复的信念。

不要用自己的各种观念和烦恼去评价他人，而要学会用静观的心来反省自己。

当人的欲望超越个人能力时，人必为欲望所累。

不要轻易伤害别人的心，因为被你伤害过的心底深处有一道残恨记忆会一直跟着你，直到你忏悔过错并不再伤人。

出现在你生命中的每一个人，都是与你有缘的人，他们同等重要。

不要因为对方的身份、地位、权力而厚此薄彼。

你的幸福不是别人给予的，而是自己创造的。

能左右你幸福的不是别人，而是你自己。

逃避只是暂缓之策，只有面对才能促进自己走向成熟。

人身体的每个器官，都是一个独立的生命体。每个生命体，又是由无数个小生命组成。

因此，我们只有学会了感恩身体内每天为自己无私奉献的各个器官和小生命，身体才会更加健康、永葆青春。

人生最大的无知是不懂惜福，没有无常观，白白把宝贵的时间浪费在吃喝享受、追求安逸中。

帮助别人不是为了得到回报，而是在这个过程中净化自己的心灵。

你在生活中给别人留有余地，其实就是给自己创造或提供生机与希望。

那些自我约束能力差，经常把不良生活习惯带到其他国家的人，所损毁的不仅是个人的形象，而是一个民族和国家的形象。

有着这种卑劣习惯，不顾及国家形象的人，与卖国贼无异。

简单是一种境界！

学会简单做事的人，其实是不简单的人。

不要因为今天没见到阳光，就认为明天还是

阴天。

不必因为没有掌声，而放弃自己的追求。

每条通往阳光的大道上，都布满艰辛与坎坷。

父母手中的权利、地位、财富是靠他们一生努力而得，千万不可成为你对外炫耀的资本。

否则，当天灾人祸降临时，你后悔晚矣。

人可以有智慧，但不可有小聪明。

喜欢耍小聪明的人，往往聪明反被聪明误。

评论事情容易，做起事情来难；做起事情来容易，做成事难。

每个人心中都有爱，但大多数人无法做到把爱播撒给所有的人。

因为，这部分人只有碰到自己的天使才会把纯粹的爱激发出来。

这里所讲的天使，就是他自己喜欢的，或者具备同一类能量场的人。

独自旅行可以增强或拓展个人生存能力和视野，二人旅行可全方位深入沟通彼此的情感，三人以上（小团队）旅行有益于加深思想的交流，十人

以上旅行完全是热闹的休闲消遣。

个人魅力的展示，不在于你是否身着名牌，而是能把普通的衣服穿出属于自己的别样味道。

尽管你知道冲动是魔鬼，可你的心总是被魔鬼掌控。

如果想远离魔鬼不再冲动，就要学会放下，不计较。不计较是防治魔鬼最善巧的方法。

一个善良干净的人，如果开始贪婪不洁之人的美色和性欲，那此人的内心就像电脑中毒一样可怕，轻者重要文件被感染，严重者会导致电脑瘫痪。

因为不洁之人的污秽之美不仅能迷乱身心，也会把贪婪情欲之欢的毒素传染给所有迷恋情色的人。

切记！

只要你有了一时性的销魂，此毒足以让你失魂

一世。

心里充满阳光，触目所及都是最美的。

即使在工作和生活中遇到挫折，心中还会保留那份阳光与热情。

善良并非懦弱，若把善良认为是懦弱，则需提高用智慧去处理各种问题的能力。

你自己的幸福感别人不会懂，别人的幸福你也一样无法理解。

所以说，幸福程度取决于自己对幸福的理解，并非取决于别人的评判。

喜欢写文章的人其实不都是写给读者看的，偶尔也是写给自己的。文章中能把自己写成主人公的其实只是少数，而在不同的时代把那些挑战命运的人写成英雄，把仗势欺人的坏人写成小丑，不仅是为了迎合当时社会大众的需要，也是慰藉心中对美好生活的期待。

遇到烦恼，不要向外寻求方案，也不要靠别人解决问题。想解决问题，就从自身找原因，从心入手，一定能找到解决你烦恼的钥匙。

请不要用行为去纵容你心里的欲望，因为欲望永远没有尽头。你越去填充欲望，内心就越深陷孤独。

无论你有多大的本事，都不要在春风得意时，瞧不起甚至伤害那些弱势群体。也许，有一天你因此而付出代价时已来不及后悔。

到农村你会发现，如一犬吠始，即会持续百犬吠声。而今，当有些别有用心的人在散布谣言、传递负面信息时，就会有一些人模仿犬的特点不加思索地跟风起哄，恶意攻击。其实，这些人真正可悲的不单单是不用脑子理性思考问题，而是助纣为虐自己还不知道。

事出必有因，乱麻必有头。今天的苦果，来自昨日的播种。当下的付出，将是明日的回报。

无论你外表多光彩照人，都不要以此为傲。因为岁月会慢慢把这些光鲜磨灭于无形。

人的爱好，要有所节制。因为你的爱好一旦形成贪欲后，就很难再回头。无形中，灾祸已离你不远。

欲如火，不抑则燎原。欲如水，不遏则滔天。欲可载舟，亦可覆舟。

只有经历生命中的风、雨、雷、电，才能普被金色光芒。

人生最大的快乐不是贪图享受，而是无私奉献。

从战场上归来的英雄从不以英雄自居，因为他知道英雄的光环是太多的战友用生命和鲜血换取的。如果有一天你载誉归来，一定不要忘记曾经和你并肩作战的战友。要是没有他们在背后默默地付出，单凭一己之力，难以取得成功和终极胜利！

山花儿虽然很美，但只可在此欣赏而不能移家种养。家中舒适的环境根本不宜山花的生长。人又何尝不是如此？

俭约可使人养成廉洁的作风，奢侈会使人贪婪成性。不论在朝做官，还是闲居乡野，如果能够节俭约束而不贪心，就可以颐养福气，使自己延年益寿。如果为官时节俭为公，则可以涵养廉洁的操守。

当你感觉不到累的时候，也许你已走过了人生的上坡路。如果你想攀登人生的另一个高度，还要继续坚持走上坡路。

每天沉浸在吃饭、交友、唱歌、跳舞的应酬里不是好事。在红尘中周旋，要时刻警觉如果再不放下享乐主义和世俗观念，你将失去自我，而且，最后的结局是你最不愿意看到的。

每个人都认为自己的生命最可贵，事实上，人与自然界中的所有生命同等珍贵。只有当地球上的生命之间确立起平等的关系，人类才有和谐美好的明天。

生活就像一个行李箱，出差时可以提起拉走，不用时再把它放下收好。如果不出差，每天也拖着沉重的行李箱来回走，你如何自在？所以，该放下的时候要坦然放下，不要执着。

无论艺术家笔下描绘的是什么，你都可以寻觅或捕捉到艺术家的灵魂。

常言道：初生牛犊不怕虎！其实不是刚刚生下的小牛犊不害怕老虎，也不是因为牛犊很勇敢，仅仅因为无知。无知者无畏，不知道后果是什么，所以不会害怕。

动物身上的肉真的会对我们的身体有滋补和保养作用吗？如果你没有亲眼目睹动物在病态下用激素喂养、临宰时极度的恐惧和痛苦，就不会把各种充满毒素的不健康肉食当做美味来享用。

“星星之火，可以燎原”。只要我们能坚持不懈地向周围的人传递温暖阳光和无私的爱心，社会一定会变得越来越和谐，每一个人都会感到越来越温暖，越来越幸福，自己的事业也会越来越兴旺。

科技是把双刃剑，既能用来做好事，也能做坏事。唯有把文明、智慧、平衡的心灵运用到科技中，才能真正造福人类。

世界不单属于某个人，而是全人类的。地球上的生命体要相互依存、相互支撑。在大自然面前，谁都没有特权可享，更不能独善其身。我们考虑个人利益之际，还要考虑社会的利益，尤其不能忽视大自然的利益。

刻意追求是过分执着。过犹不及，过分的执着有时候会造成无法挽回的伤害。所以，对有些事情，我们无须强求，无须刻意。我们虽然没办法改

变命运，但是只要能保住一份宁静的心态，不去执着，生活会日益吉祥圆满。

当你把西方国家的糟粕当作精华来欺骗善良的中国人时，其实你已成为最大的受害者与造业者。

无论是周公解梦，还是科学家对梦的预测，都无法破解你在梦中的无名，所谓解梦和预测的结果只是对你执着梦境的一种慰藉。

当你把所有精力放在镜子前欣赏和描画自己那张脸时，要意识到大家未必是欣赏你画出来的容颜，也许你的素颜美更具有魅力。

海到天边天做岸，山登绝顶我为峰。站得高看

得远！阳光可以瞬间从云海里喷射出光芒，让人叹为观止，亦能够长久隐藏起来教我们从容立世。

国家不是一个人的家，是天下人的家。无论国家还是小家，都需要我们大家自觉维护。外出游玩时，请主动承担起一个公民的责任，时刻树立阳光形象，传递文明信息，做到文明出行，我们的旅途才能平安快乐。因为，我们的一言一行都影响着整个社会。

“贪污”出自《庄子•秋水》，意为贪利忘义。永远不要试图贪污国家的财产，因为里面承载着全国人民的血和汗。凡敢将国家财产中饱私囊者，将为此付出沉重的代价。吾辈确信没有人可以凌驾于法律与道义之上！

世上没有完美的人，只有完美的梦想。事事追求完美的人，会认为给裸露土地撒满草籽发芽后就再也看不到小草下面的土坑，却不知走近草地，那土坑依旧清楚可见。

不要一味低头为生活奔忙，偶尔也要学会适度停歇。“忙=心+亡”，拆解后的两个字已告诉你此中真意，如果心迷失了就只剩下穷忙了。要关注身心健康和乐享生活真味，勿舍本逐末。

在这个喧嚣的城市背后，每个人内心深处，都是沉默的、孤独的……孤独，是心灵的静默独舞；孤独，是冉冉黎明后的再次轮回；孤独，是浸润柔软心境的清水。不必惧怕或躲避孤独，要发掘它的深意。

日历是一本时光纪念册，翻过去的日子已成为历史，剩下的每一页都是我们即将面对的未来。岁月的意韵，在我们翻阅的指尖流淌。

墙头上的草儿虽然扎根在高地，其实未必能经受风霜侵凌。不管身居何处，自身的薄弱注定它会枯萎先凋。

当你从梦境中醒来时，请不要再执着于昨天所做的梦。因为，无论梦的好坏都无法改变你当下的生活。你醒了吗？

即使我是一缕微弱的阳光，也要将温暖和光亮

播撒到需要它的地方。

清晨幸福地醒来，是看到你和阳光都在，那就是我想要的最近和最好的未来！

无论是错过还是过错，如果确已无法重来或者弥补，那么最好的出路就是吸取教训，义无反顾继续向前！

无论是谁，不管财富、权利、地位多么显赫，或者曾为人类和国家做出多少贡献，请不要居功自傲。因为你也会因病而疾，到老而终。当你无法为社会奉献，会有人来代替你，这就是自然规律。

负面情绪如不及时清除，日积月累必让你为此所累。要想心里永葆光明，请随时删除当下的不开心。

愚公要是当年不移山，而是带家人迁移到一个

最适合他们的环境去生活，后人都不知道愚公是谁。

当你向国家和人民伸手寻求帮助时，请先扪心自问你为国家、人民做过多少贡献。

喜欢户外运动的人，比只在室内滞留的人更健康。

无论做公益、慈善还是帮朋友做事儿，建议量力而行，千万不要碍于情面打肿脸充胖子，如果勉为其难，会使双方陷入僵局，同时带给自己和周围的人无尽烦恼。

人无论拥有多少财富、荣誉，一旦背离了道德、法律的轨道，等待他的将是追悔莫及的铁窗人生。

列车启动，远离繁华只是瞬间的感受。列车人生般地在站台停留、开动。列车可以晚点，但你的生命不允许晚点。你该在哪一站下都已安排好，不是你陪伴其他旅客，就是其他旅客陪伴你，但是走向终点的只有你一个人。

当你感觉无助的时候，请不要拒绝众人的爱心帮助。你的接受是对爱心人士最好的回馈。接受帮助本身也是打开自己了解和接纳外界的过程，社会和谐需要更多互助和爱心传递！

公益或者慈善不仅仅局限于经济和物质上的资助，更大的意义是帮助对方走出身心困境，让受助人变得更有信心和力量，同时使他变成一颗火种，把接受到的爱复制成更多份继续传递下去。

什么是阅历？阅历就是教会我们把复杂的事情化繁为简、变难为易。

有时候，眼见不一定为实。如果你只相信从个人的角度所看到的一切，仅凭经验与直觉妄下结论，不但会与事物的全貌失之交臂，而且轻率得出的结论只会是空中楼阁，沙上建塔，立不住。

一张人民币掉进污水沟，再找回来绝不会贬值，一页白纸掉进去再捞上来就是废纸。人生如同一张洁净的白纸，在成长中每个人却各自描绘不同的画面，或阳光，或晦暗；或高尚，或猥琐；或善良，或丑恶。每个人应该用心将人生的白纸绘出绚丽独特的画面，否则将如同污水沟里的废纸，虽生犹亡。

从容走过，你恍然发现自己忽略的不是陪你共同成长的阳光和雨露，而是花丛里的那些小草。

当你每天为工作和生活累得疲惫不堪时，不必抱怨压力太大，而是暂时放慢步履，静心沉淀。

无论多么娇艳的鲜花都会凋零，无论多么美丽的叶子都会枯萎，无论多么娇俏的容颜都会老去，无论多么优秀的自己终有后人超越……请谨记和接受宇宙的前进法则：活在当下、爱在当下、传递阳光大爱在当下。

高温高不过人的热情，低温低不过冷漠的心。

给你设置障碍的人未必是坏人，也许是你有意识或无意识的言行冒犯了对方才会有此障碍。常常，人生各个阶段出现的障碍是一味药，专治各种自满、骄傲和自以为是。

不要因为自己的出身、外表、学历而自卑，正因为你的存在，才会让一些人找到自己的“位置”。

孩子的考试能力无论有多好，若道德缺失，对父母而言都是教育的失败。

遇到困难越害怕，困难就像杂草一样杂乱纷芜，把你团团围住，无法呼吸。若把困难视为增上缘，这些杂草就像一道特别的风景，独具意味。

生命里没有如果只有无常，只要敢于面对无常，所有的如果皆有可能。

小说、电视剧无论有多吸引人都不可过度痴迷。当你在虚构故事情节里大喜大悲时，身体也会因此损耗精气。

鱼遇水则欢，芙蓉遇知己则荣，人遇贵人则兴。

云散水流去，寂然天地空。以平常心处事，如行云流水，回归本真，参透人生。

清净无为，万物自成。

春雨虽好，不润无根之草，中医虽妙，难医不信之人。

眼睛虽小，可以看遍世界。鼻孔虽小，能嗅着虚空的气息。细胞虽小，却是生命的支点。小善虽小，却能让你厚德载物。

突如其来的诽谤犹如一口不小心飞溅脸颊的唾沫，越在乎那唾沫的腥味就越难受，不理它反而会自己蒸发。

人人皆有美之处，从内至外所流露的是内涵之美，能让人记忆犹新，如沐春风。从外到内所表现的不是纯正之美，而多矫揉造作或粉饰，会让轻浮者迷失心性，让君子逃之夭夭。

当你的德行与福报成正比时，无论你是否努

力，财富都会如影随行地跟着你。

不要把生活安排得太满，多空余一点空间才不会缺氧。

计划可以改变，人生可以改变，性情也可以改变，唯独历史无法改变。

生活在高空的人缺少踏实平稳的安全感，而地面的人总是羡慕着高空的生活。

在时间的长河里什么都留不下，你执着一个人、一间屋、一件东西又有什么意义？爱是祝福，不是贪欲。真爱无私，假爱贪杯。只有放下假爱才能看清真爱，真爱不在角落里，其实就在你的心里。

无论你是否与我相伴，我依然在成长。也许我们就此相别，那在风中摇曳的影子已成为时间的乐谱。不要留恋过去，现在才是最真实的自己。我留不是为了明天，我走不是为了今朝。无

论去留都在时间的轨道里。

你的心我看不到，但你的呼吸我能听到。你的模样我看不到，可你的磁场我能感受到。你有所想，我有所不想。你在水中畅游，我在空与非空里翱翔。

没有压力的爱才是人人都向往的爱，如果两个人在一起压力大于爱，那一定是你们的选择存在问题。

有人的地方就有矛盾，有矛盾的地方就有真理，有真理的地方就有真假、好坏、对错。当心中没有矛的时候，就不会出现盾。当不需要盾的时候，矛就很难出现在你的面前。

人间最远的距离莫过于相识之后的陌生。

德高者习惯体谅人，无德者喜好抱怨人。

医生给患者治病是希望患者康复，而非蜻蜓赏花只求自安。医患之间的信任是治疗的根本。

可以存钱，但存不了时间。可以借钱，但借不来时间。

真正的爱情不在节日里，而在日常生活的点点滴滴。

在这世界上，无论是谁，人生都如昙花一现，终将回归尘土。所以，趁你的昙花还未开时多做无私利他的事情。也许，就因此善举，你这朵昙花有可能会延迟开放。

花开花落天知晓，潮起潮落有多少？人的一生犹如日月星辰起落有序，只要不脱离自然规律，在正确的轨道上运行你就必能成就一番事业。

最美的世界里有最美的你不是神话，因为它在每个人的心里。生活、工作环境会无常变化，但简单而纯粹的心恒久美好。

读书明智，读圣贤书可知万物之理，尽千古之远。

拜明师学艺固然重要，但如果没有基础，找到明师指点也如空中楼阁，难于真正领会提升。

有一种图片工具可以改变很多人的“美”。美颜后还是真实的你吗？也许早已分不清真正的你在哪里。

心病，则需心药医。若用错药，则全盘皆错。

在成长的路上不怕一无所获，就怕迷失航向后

找不到自己。

越简单的话越值得回味，越简单的事越难做到极致，人往往追求复杂的完美而忽视简单的魅力。

不能破“执”，就难于接受良言善语。心中没有智慧，就难于真正“放下”。

生命的延续在于运动，而非被动。

有一种情不是相爱相守，而是寄情于你我，没有世俗的姻缘，寄情就是最好的选择。

最真实的语言是无言，只要心心相应无需赘语。

人生最大的乐趣不是获取，而是奉献。当从无私奉献中找到自己的人生价值时，这种乐趣是他人无法体会的。

用真心陪你工作和生活的，定是心中有爱之人。对这样的人，一定悉心去珍惜。否则，失去不复得之。

有一种悄无声息的温暖就是父母对孩子的爱，如果人人都能把这种温暖传递在世间每一个角落，那世间的灾害就会悄然而止。

懈怠是慢性毒药，待明白为时晚矣。

不管昨天如何，今天一定要活出自己。这，才是最真实的人生。

看重名利则会被名利所伤，淡泊名利则不易被名利所左右。

真正的美人不仅仅是外表美，而是内外兼修的美。内心善良，为人谦和，做事利他，散发真正的美。

人这一生，十有八九不如意。辉煌时，如日中天，夕阳西下，落日后余晖也随之幻灭。若看破禅机，在一池残荷中享受孤老的自在，在无所得和无所失中体悟生命静谧之美。

不必把所有人都请进生命里，生命归根到底是一场不能与他人同行的独自修行。不过，能请进生命里的那些人，虽未必是当下最合适的人，但至少是在某个阶段最重要的人。正因为他们的存在，充盈了你的人生。一生一次芳华，无法留住最美的瞬间，能忆起的只是过往。走吧！不要缠绵于欲望的幻想。无论和谁在一起，都是孤独的旅途。路上所有的人和事都是修行的助缘。

有梦想的人在努力付出后，或许未到达理想的彼岸，但至少会因此闯出禁锢自己的森林。连梦想都没有的人，注定在平庸中被岁月的风尘所埋没。

经济困难不可怕，怕的是心穷。因为心穷的人看不到他人的好与善良，只在意自己的得失。若需要你帮助的时候，他就是一团热情的火。当向他稍稍提出要求，他就是一块坚硬的冰。

文字有时是虚假的，只有亲身经历过才是真实的。

有人说在这个世界上，能永远陪伴你的，只有你自己。其实，真正爱你的人无论在不在你身边都时刻用心在陪伴着你。

当局限于小圈子思考问题时，只会关注得失。若能跳出圈子去思考问题，会发现世界竟然海阔天空的辽远。

陪伴是爱的一种方式，那种无声胜有声的爱虽无言，却很纯粹。

人生可以没有高度，但不能没有温度。也许你喜欢平凡，无需高度；只要心存感恩，时时不忘传递爱心和微笑，温度就会慢慢抬高你的高度。

真金需火炼，好荷泥中生；真火炼就金之明，淤泥养育荷之净。此乃天地因缘之法则，心敬则明也。

富有的人不喜欢炫耀自己的富，有才华的人不显摆自己的才，有能力不自夸自己的能。而缺少自信、底气不足、爱面子的人反而喜欢借用他人的名气、财富、能力去抬高自己。

如果荷花抱怨淤泥减损了自己的美丽，她并非真正的高雅清洁。如果总是抱怨自己的家庭、工作不好，那你将失去整个世界。

对未知的体触不一定是真实的，但一定是认知世界的开始。

庄子认为，真正自由之人，不被自己的本能

欲望所控制，顺应自然之变化，不受名利的诱惑，不丧失自然本性，就如同化身为一只蝴蝶，自由不羁，摆脱社会加在个人身上的各种“身份”束缚，生如蚁而美如神！

人不怕有梦想，但不可活在梦里无法自拔。

福是修来的，而不是求来的。

靠虚伪和谎言所得到的任何东西，最终将会因正气和真实而毁其所有。

老物件无论真伪，只要能传世，足说明此物有特别之处。只要你心中认为是最好的，又何必在乎它本身的真伪。

越是喜欢的东西越不能贪，因为不理智的喜欢恰恰是断送你前程和命运的考题。

真正快乐的人，他们的人生其实多半不是“加法”，而是“减法”。因为，愈是脱去繁琐外在的雕饰，让自己露出纯粹的本心，愈能得到身心的安宁。

人活在世上，有的活成了面子，有的活成了里子。而只有里子，才能赢得真正的面子。幸福是真实的，面子是虚无的。不要让幸福输给薄薄的面子，一点一滴都不行。

不付诸行动的理想永远像空中楼阁一样让你生

活在幻境，难以看到真实的世界。

天地长久亘古不变。它们之所以能够持久存在，原因在于它们的存在不是为了自己。

It is not fearful that you have desires; it is fearful, however, if you lose self-control when desires arrive.

Less care for gains and losses, rather than ample possession, enables the broad-minded to enjoy their life.

Not getting off at one's arrival at the high-speed train station is like moving away from life's goal. If you keep moving forward, you will get further away from your destination, and only walking back will take you to the right way.

The number of the audience depends on the size of the stage. So does your ability. Without the audience's generous support, you will have to exit; without the stage to support your ability, you are destined to fail or remain in obscurity.

Apart from the hidden merit accumulated by their ancestors, people can also benefit from being grateful and passing on love. On the contrary, if they only seek a life of pleasure, never care about karma and do no good, they will be out of luck after running out of their ancestors' blessing.

Those who always consider themselves perfect tend to lose themselves in their narcissism.

Life experiences are written on one's face, while the life story is covered in history.

Life disappears in a twinkling, in which the very destiny you desire for is hard to obtain.

Whether good or bad, you have to cherish your destiny, let it be, but don't play up to it, because all destinies rely on your momentary decisions.

It is wise to align with destiny but foolish to embrace casualness.

The former enables you to keep calm and face your business correctly, while the latter will make you ignorant of rules and easily spell trouble or even disaster.

The biggest harvest in life is not to achieve success alone, but to find a person who understands you to accompany you through all of life's experiences till you're old in age.

Happiness is not derived from your status or wealth, but from your inner abundance and satisfaction.

Do not hate your body or be upset by your appearance due to its inferiority to others'. Our environments are created by our thoughts. Appearance can be changed because of our cultivation; temperament can be improved because of the environment.

In life, there are too many things that people are willing or unwilling to do, to have and to love.

Instead of struggling against them, it is better to accept with a calm heart what we cannot change, change what we can, and make a breakthrough in our inner world.

Then there will be more happiness and sweetness, and less trouble and bitterness in your life.

There is no suffering in the world. You are unable to get rid of it only because you hold things too tight and haven't learned to let go.

Things change with time. When you look back later, you'll find that nothing matters.

The materials people need for survival are very limited, but their desires are unlimited.

Excessive pursuit of material pleasure will make them slaves of desires.

It is the responsibility of not only the government and the environmental protection department but also every citizen to reduce and control haze.

If everyone can act consciously to care for and protect the environment and the earth, the haze will clear away itself.

If you find small faults in others, you should first reflect on the same ones in yourself, and then accept theirs. If you find serious faults in others, you should first learn lessons from them, and then give them a timely suggestion in plain words with sincerity to correct their faults.

Stay at a respectful distance from those who do not have good morality even if they are older than you; pay your earnest respect

to those who have good virtue even if they are younger than you.

The best way to cultivate one's field of fortune is not to burn incense or kowtow, but to adhere to the original frugality, no matter how one's material life changes.

Your greed, anger and ignorance can be seen by others, while your jealousy and arrogance may not be recognized at once even by yourself, let alone others.

The physical suffering is temporary, while the mental one is life-long.

To avoid the latter, you must get rid of your greed, anger, ignorance, arrogance, and doubt.

When you are surrounded by darkness, do not blindly complain about alienation and indignation. First, please seek the sunshine in your inner world, and shine the light of mercy around with the goodwill at the bottom of your heart.

In the eyes of the selfless, everyone is precious and unique, and has the equal innate potential of kindness and selflessness.

Once controlled by desire, people will become its slaves; otherwise, they will become the masters of their lives.

Do not unlimitedly pursue material pleasure in your own world.

Once all you covet runs out, your soul, which is still dissatisfied by materials, will suffer greatly.

Do not blindly pursue a greater happiness and lose your original happiness.

In fact, inner abundance is the greatest true wealth of life.

There are too many people pursuing profits, few of whom can actually be rich.

Instead, the low-key and humble, who love to share their blessings with others, have a better reputation.

Poverty is caused not only by laziness, but also by parsimony and selfishness.

If you want to be rich, you must have a broad mind.

When you really try to help for the interests of others rather than your own, wealth will favor you!

In this world, the one who can grant you health, safety and happiness is not anyone else, but the wise and kind heart you are born with.

If being trusted is a kind of happiness, trusting others can also be a chance of having one more way to happiness.

It is difficult for the suspicious to make true friends.

It is easy to practice philanthropy once, but difficult for a lifetime.

If all you do every day can benefit others, it will not be difficult to do so for a lifetime.

Happiness is not given by others, but won by yourself.

Because you know best about whether you are happy or not.

In daily life, no one is naturally responsible for helping you.

When you need help, be thankful for others no matter whether their help counts or not.

Never hold a grudge against them even if they offer no help.

Know "it is what it is" when you are sick.

Treat everyone and everything with sincerity, and you will accordingly enjoy better health as your mentality changes for the better. Just as the saying goes, things will be more interesting if done unhurriedly; one lives longer if calm.

Never regard the suffering you have as the fault of others. In fact, all your emotions such as joy, anger, sorrow and happiness, are caused by yourself.

When you look up to others, someone else actually does the same to you.

Instead of looking at the success of others, you'd better appreciate the present.

Mistakes are not horrible unless made once again after being realized.

As long as your heart is full of sunshine, it will not grow old no matter how old time grows.

Obstacles can be everywhere in daily life. If you don't objectively examine your own problems and merely blame fate or others, you will definitely experience an ending more serious than you expected.

If someone else slanders you, reflect on yourself first, as there must be some reasons that gave him the opportunity to do so.

The plots of all movies and TV dramas are nothing but stories that combine imagination and reality. So do not indulge too much in them and lose yourself; otherwise, blind following and imitating would hurt yourself as well as others.

People with a pure heart find no shortcomings in others, while those without it, whatever faults they have themselves, they will always see the faults in others.

The power and wealth obtained around us are not real blessings. It is the rich spirit that won't be influenced by the variable destinies.

People will encounter a lot of questions in life, but not all of them necessarily have answers.

In fact, instead of only concerning yourself with the answers, you should ensure yourself that peace and happiness are more important.

God grants you a beautiful appearance, which enables the world to appreciate your beauty.

God favors you with a heart of universal love, which gives off sunshine and illuminates every corner of the land.

Your beauty and love will always be in the world.

Those who do not often write, if sent a fan and asked to write on it, can't do as well as usual, because they expect to succeed and worry too much.

In fact, excessive worries and desire for success often lead to a failure.

When some hot news is publicized maliciously on the Internet, please think rationally and do not blindly follow up or forward those posts.

In fact, the hot news is used by some people only to obtain benefits.

Keep calm no matter what affects your life, blessings or misfortunes.

At this point, if you can't control your emotions well, you will become a slave to them.

The benefits and significance of a vegetarian diet have nothing to do with the pursuit of fashion or personal beliefs.

When you truly participate in it, you will find what you have is a harmonious, safe and reliable food culture.

To remove scars and hatred, the best way is not to insist on revenge but change the environment for your heart so that those nameless troubles can be reduced.

You can never satisfy everyone all the time, so don't please others at the expense of your nature. Besides, people who appreciate you will always support you!

Do not reflect on usual ignorance of your health only after

falling ill.

When someone else is ill, your smile and greeting are enough to support their faith in a quick recovery.

Do not evaluate others with your own ideas and frustrations. Instead, learn to examine yourself with a peaceful heart.

You will get tired when your desire exceeds your capability.

Do not easily hurt the hearts of others; otherwise, the remaining memory of hatred at the bottom of those hearts will always follow you until you confess and promise not to hurt others anymore.

Everyone appearing in your life has affinity with you and is of the most importance to you.

Do not treat them with partiality due to their identity, social status or rights.

Your happiness is not granted by others but created by yourself.

Control of your happiness does not lie with others, but rather with you.

Escape is nothing but a temporary strategy, and the only way to help you mature is to confront your problems.

Every organ of a human body is an independent life entity, which also consists of countless little lives.

Therefore, only when we learn to thank the organs and little lives in our bodies for their selfless dedication every day, can we become healthier and remain youthful.

The biggest ignorance of life is not cherishing fortune and having no concept of impermanence, wasting valuable time in food, drink and the pursuit of ease.

To help others is not to expect something in return, but to purify your heart in this process.

When you give leeway to others in daily life, you actually leave hope for yourself.

Those, who have poor self-restraint and often bring undesirable habits to other countries, damage the images of not only themselves but also their nations and countries.

Those with such despicable habits regardless of the national images are hardly different from traitors.

Simplicity is a state.

People learning to do things in a simple way are far from being simple.

Do not think it will be cloudy tomorrow only because you did not see the sun today.

Do not give up your pursuit because of the lack of applause.

Every road to sunshine is filled with hardships and frustrations.

You shouldn't show off the rights, status and wealth your parents have obtained with their lifetime's efforts.

Otherwise, it will be too late for regret when disasters happen.

People can have wisdom, but not cleverness in trivial matters.

People who like to fool others often fall victim to their own cleverness.

Talking is easy, but taking action is hard, and succeeding in that business even harder.

Everyone has love in his/her hearts, but most people cannot

pass on their love to everyone.

Only when they encounter their angels will their pure love be stimulated.

The angels mentioned here refer to those they like or share the same energy field with.

Travelling alone can increase and expand your personal viability and perspectives; travelling with another one enables you to get to know and be close with each other thoroughly and emotionally; travelling with another two or more can benefit in-depth exchange of ideas; and travelling with nine and more people is absolutely lively and leisurely.

Personal charm doesn't depend on the branded clothes you are dressed in, but your own style in ordinary clothes.

You do know that impulse is a devil, but your heart is always controlled by it.

If you want to stay away from it and not be impulsive anymore, you must learn to let go and not fuss over anything, as it is the best way to prevent the devil from taking control.

If a good and pure person begins to desire beauty and sex of the impure, his heart will suffer as a computer does when infected by a virus, which leads to the corruption of important files or even a crash.

The unclean beauty of the impure not only bewilders us physically and mentally, but also infects all those who are addicted to vices.

Do keep it in mind!

As long as you have a temporary ecstasy of sex, this virus is enough to make you lost for the rest of your life.

Fill your heart with sunshine, and you will see nothing but the most beautiful things.

Even if you encounter obstacles in work or daily life, you can still retain the sunshine and enthusiasm in your heart.

Goodness is not cowardice. If misunderstanding this, you should enhance your ability to deal with various problems through wisdom.

Others cannot understand your happiness and vice versa.

Therefore, our happiness depends on our understanding of it, instead of what other people's judgement.

People who love writing will not only write for readers, but also for themselves. The leading characters in literature works are seldom the writer. The writers usually shape the ill-fated people into heroes and the bullies into knaves. By doing so they can not only cater to the need of the society in that time, but also console their yearning for a better life.

When you are annoyed, do not find solutions outside of you; nor should you rely on others to solve the problem. To tackle it you should reflect on yourself from the bottom of your heart, and the key to solving the problem will surely be found.

Please do not indulge your heart in desires, since they will never be satisfied. The more you desire, the lonelier your heart will be.

No matter how capable you are, you can't look down upon or even hurt the vulnerable when you are riding on the crest of success. Maybe one day, you will have to pay the price and it will be too late to regret.

As the saying goes, "one dog barks at a shadow and one hundred dogs bark at the sound". Now, when some people spread rumors and negative information with an ulterior motive, there will always be others to follow the trend without hesitation, just like the dogs who bark at the sound. In fact, what is truly pitiful of them is not their thoughtlessness, but their aiding and abetting the evil.

Everything has its cause. The outcome today is the result of yesterday's sowing. Today's pain will be tomorrow's gain.

No matter how gorgeous you are, you should not be arrogant because beauty will fade as time goes.

People's interests should be moderated. As soon as interests turn into lust, it will be difficult for you to turn back. At this point, disaster is not far away from you.

Desire is like fire; if not controlled, it will become a prairie fire. Desire is like water; if not controlled, it will become a flood. The desire, like water, can sink ships as well as keep them afloat.

Only when you have gone through the "wind", "rain", "thunder" and "lightening" in your life can you see the golden sunshine.

The greatest happiness in life is not to indulge in a life of pleasure and comfort, but to make contributions selflessly.

The soldiers returning from the battlefield never call themselves heroes, because they know how much blood and how many lives of their comrades it cost to be a hero. If one day you return home with honor, you should not forget the comrades you fought with. If they hadn't had your back, you wouldn't have succeeded on your own.

Although the wildflowers are beautiful, they can only be appreciated rather than moved to your house. While houses are comfortable, the indoor environment in is not suitable for them. Isn't it the same with human beings?

Being frugal can help people develop a clean working style, while being extravagant makes people greedy. Whether you are an official or not, as long as you can stay frugal and not greedy, you can enjoy and prolong your life. If you can stay frugal and always have the public's interest in mind when you are an official, you can develop integrity.

When you don't feel tired anymore, maybe that means you have already passed the upward slope of your life. If you want to

reach another height, you will need to walk up another upward slope.

It's not good to keep yourself busy every day with social engagements like dining out, making friends, singing and dancing. Therefore, you must remind yourself constantly that you need to put down the hedonism and the secular concepts; otherwise you will lose yourself, and the final outcome will be the last thing you want to see.

It's common that everyone thinks his own life is precious, but only a few people will think all the other living creatures' lives are precious too. Only when there is an equal relationship between all life on the earth, can human beings have a truly beautiful future.

Life is like a suitcase which you take with on a business trip and put away when you don't need it. You can't be free if you carry a heavy suitcase around when you don't need it. So, you should put it down when necessary. Don't be too obstinate.

Whatever an artist depicts in his work, you will see or find the artist's soul.

As the saying goes, "the newborn calf isn't afraid of tigers." It's not because the newborn calf is not really afraid of the tigers, nor is it very brave, but because of its ignorance. It is fearless because of the ignorance. Not knowing the consequences makes it fearless.

Can animal's meat really nourish and maintain our body? If you ever saw the animals being fed with hormones, and their extreme fear and pain when being butchered, you will not view the unhealthy meat as a delicacy to enjoy.

Sparks can start a prairie fire. As long as we can pass the warm sunshine and selfless love to the people around, the whole society will become more and more harmonious. Everyone will feel warmer and warmer, and happier and happier. They will also become more and more prosperous.

Science and technology is a double-edged sword, which can be used in both good and bad ways. Only when civil, wise and balanced minds utilize science and technology can it truly benefit mankind.

The world is not for one person, but for all. We live on the Earth where we need to rely on and support each other. Faced with nature, no one can get privilege or stand aloof. Therefore, we should not only consider our own interests, but also the interests of society, and especially those of nature.

It is too excessive to pursue something deliberately. Going

beyond the limit is as bad as falling short. Sometimes going too far will cause irreparable damage. So, we do not have to insist on some certain things. We can't change fate, but as long as we can maintain peaceful minds and stop being obsessive, we can live better lives.

When you consider the dross of western countries to be fundamental and deceive the kind-hearted Chinese people, you have already become the biggest victim and wrong-doer.

Neither the Chinese traditional interpretation of dreams nor scientific interpretations can explain the unknowns in your dreams. The so-called dream interpretations and forecasts can only console yourself.

When you put on makeup in front of the mirror and appreciate your face, you need to know that what others like may not be your makeup. Maybe your natural beauty is more attractive.

When the sea comes to an end, the sky will be the shore; and when you climb to the top of the mountain, you will be the peak. The higher you stand, the further you can see! When sunshine glows, it will be breathtaking; when it hides, you can live a peaceful life.

Our country is not one person's home, but the home for us all. With either a big country or a small home, we need to work together to maintain it. When going on a trip abroad, each of us needs to take the responsibility to establish a good image and pass on our culture. Green and courteous travel can make our journey peaceful and happy. Because each word and action of ours can influence the whole society.

"Corruption", deriving from "Zhuangzi", means forgetting honor for profit. We should never have the attempt to embezzle the country's property, because it carries the blood and sweat of the people nationwide. Whoever dares to fill his own pocket with public funds will eventually pay a heavy price. Our generation believes that no one can overtop the law and morality!

There is no perfect person, but only perfect dreams. Those who seek perfection think that bare land can be covered with seedlings to hide holes in the land, only find out that the holes can still clearly be seen when walked up close to.

Don't bow to the bustle in life; you should stop and rest from time to time. The word busy in Chinese is "忙" in which the "忄" means "heart" and "亡" means "death." This tells the truth: if your heart is dead, being busy accomplishes nothing. Pay attention to physical and mental health and enjoy life. Don't forget what the root of your life is.

Behind the hustle and bustle of the city, everyone's heart is

silent and lonely. Loneliness is a solo dance of the soul, the rising reincarnation after the dawn, and the clean water moistening your heart. Do not be afraid of loneliness or avoid it, find deeper meaning within it.

A calendar is a journey log book-yesterday has become history, and the rest of the book is the future we are about to face. The taste of life flows through our fingers as we turn the pages.

Grass may take root on the top of a wall, but it may not be able to withstand the icy wind. So, it is doomed to wither first.

When waking up, you should try not to be immersed in the dream you had yesterday. Whether the dream is good or bad, it can't change your present life. Are you awake?

Even if I were only a wisp of faint sunshine, I will spread the warmth and light into each corner in need.

The happiest moment waking up in the morning is when I can see you with the sunshine. That is the nearest and best future I want to see.

If you have already missed something or made a mistake, and can't start over again or make up, then the best way out will be learning the lesson and moving forward!

No matter who you are, regardless of your wealth, power, status, and the contributions you have made to mankind and the country, you can't take any credit for yourself or be proud. Since you will be sick and old, when you no longer dedicate your life to people, someone of a higher level will replace you, which is the law of nature.

If you don't release your negative feelings in time, you will burden yourself gradually. If you want to be optimistic forever, you should free yourself from the current unhappiness.

If the Foolish Man who tried to move the mountain in front of his house had never tried to do so, but rather moved to a place more suitable for his family to live, maybe none of us would know who he is today.

Before reaching out to the country and people for help, you should first ask yourself how many contributions you have made for the country and people.

People who like outdoor sports are always healthier than those who only exercise indoors.

Whether for performing philanthropy or helping friends, you should do it according to your own ability. If you bite off more than you can chew, you'll reach a deadlock and bring yourself and the people around you endless troubles.

No matter how much wealth or honor you have, once you deviate from morality or law, a regretful life behind bars will await you.

When setting off along with the train, you are just getting away from the bustling city life for a moment. The train stops and leaves, just like a life. The train may be late, but your life will not be allowed to. Your destination is settled, so you either accompany other passengers or get accompanied by them, but only you can head towards your destination.

Do not refuse the help from others when you feel helpless, because your acceptance of love is the best reward to those helping you. Acceptance itself is the process of opening up to the outside world, since social harmony requires more mutual assistance and sharing of love!

Public welfare or charity should not be limited to economic and material assistance. It is more important to help others get out of the troubles of physical and mental health to become stronger and more confident. This will simultaneously turn them into a spark so they can pass on the love they have received.

What is experience? It is how to teach us to make complex things simple and difficult things easy.

Sometimes, seeing is not believing. If you only believe what you have seen and draw conclusions from your experience and instinct, you will miss the opportunity to see the whole picture, and such reckless conclusion will only be a castle in the air, or a tower in the sand, which cannot stand.

When picked up after falling into a ditch, a banknote will not be devalued, while a blank sheet of paper will turn into waste.

Life is like a clean sheet of paper, but each of us will draw our own paintings ourselves as we grow up; and the paintings could be optimistic or pessimistic, noble or wretched, and kind or ugly. Each person should carefully draw the picture of their life as brilliantly and uniquely as they can, otherwise life will be as meaningless as the ruined paper in the ditch.

When you have peacefully gone through your life, you will suddenly find out what you have ignored is not the sunshine and the rain that have accompanied you, but the grass under the flowering shrubs.

If you feel exhausted by your daily work and life, don't complain about pressure, but persuade yourself that it's okay to slow down.

No matter how beautiful the flowers and leaves are, they will wither; no matter how tender the face is, it will age; no matter how excellent you are, you will be surpassed by the later generation. Remember and accept the laws of the universe: live in the present, love in the present, and spread love in the present.

Nothing is warmer than a person's warmth; nothing is colder than an indifferent heart.

Those who set roadblocks for you may not necessarily be bad people. Perhaps it was because your actions or words, intentional or unintentional, offended them. Often, the roadblocks in life are good medicine that treat arrogance, pride and self-conceit.

Do not feel inferior because of your birth, appearance, or

education. Because of your existence, others can find their own "position".

Regardless how well a child can do in a test, if he is lacking in virtues, it is a failure of education to the parents.

The more scared you are when encountering difficulties, the more difficult it is for you to breath. Hardship, like a weed, will surround you and choke you. If you regard the difficult situation as an opportunity to grow, then the weed can also become a unique scenery with its own special meaning.

There are no "ifs" in life but impermanence. So long as you are brave to face the impermanence, all the "ifs" can turn into possibilities.

Do not overindulge in novels or TV shows, no matter how attractive the stories are. When your emotions experience the deep ups-and-downs of these made-up stories, your body and heath can also lose it vitality.

A fish is happy in water and flowers appear more beautiful when appreciated. Likewise, a person will do better when there is someone to help.

As the clouds disperse and water flows away, nothing is permanent. Like floating clouds and running water, we return to our true selves and experience life's true meaning.

With a pure mind and no desires, things will happen naturally.

The timely spring rain cannot nourish rootless grass; the best Chinese traditional medicine cannot treat those who do not believe.

Though small, the eyes can see the world, the nose can smell the air, and the cells can support all of life. Similarly, the smallest kind act can result in the biggest virtue.

Unexpected slander arrives as though careless spit sticks onto your face. The more you are annoyed by the smell of the spit, the more uncomfortable you become. Ignored, it will evaporate.

It is human nature to love beauty. True meaningful beauty, coming from the inside, is memorable; while manufactured and pretentious beauty, coming from the outside, dazzles the frivolous and keeps the gentleman away.

When your virtue is proportional to your blessing, fortune will follow you whether you try or not.

Do not arrange your life too full; leaving a little space prevents you from being suffocated.

Plans can change, so can lives and temperaments, but not history.

Those who live high above lack the feeling of security; those who live on the ground always envy the life high above.

Nothings stays as times flows. How meaningful it is to be attached to a person, a house or a thing? Love is to wish good luck, not greed. True love is selfless; false love is excessive. Not until you let go of the false love can you see true love, which is nowhere else but in your heart.

I continue to grow with or without you. Perhaps we will depart now leaving the shadow in the wind to punctuate the passing of time. Do not yearn for the past, for the you of today is the real you. My staying is not for tomorrow; my departure is not for today. All is in the track of time…

I cannot see your heart, but I can hear your breathing. I cannot see your appearance, but I can feel your energy. You have your thoughts; I have mine. You enjoy a good swim in the water while I soar in the sky.

The love that comes with no pressure is the love people seek. If there is more pressure than love, then you have a problem.

Where there are humans, there are conflicts. Where there are conflicts, there is truth. Where there is truth, there is real and fake, good and bad, and right and wrong. When there are no conflicts in your heart, conflicts will cease from outside. And when you do not need conflicts, they will rarely confront you.

The longest distance between two people is the estrangement after knowing each other.

Those with virtue tend to tolerateothers; those without virtue complain about others.

Doctors hope to heal patients, not seeking self-fame. The trust between a doctor and patient is the root to healing.

Saving money is possible, but not saving time. Borrowing money is possible, but not borrowing time.

True love does not exist only during holidays, but in the mundane of daily life.

In this world, life is a flash in the pan no matter who you are – All goes back to dust. So, before the flower fades, do more selfless deeds to benefit others. Perhaps because of such a kind act, the flower of your life will bloom longer.

As flowers bloom and spend, waves come and go. A person's life is as orderly as the sunrise and sunset. As long as you follow nature's law and set foot on the right path, you will be destined to succeed.

It is not a fairytale that in the most beautiful world exists the most beautiful you because the most beautiful world is in everyone's

heart. Your life and work environment will change, but the simple and pure heart remains beautiful forever.

Reading enlightens wisdom. By reading books written by the sage, you can understand true wisdom.

Learning from the most achieved teachers is important; however, without the foundation, even if you find the teacher, you can hardly make progress, just like a castle in the air.

A photo application can beautify a person. But is that the real you? Perhaps you can no longer distinguish where the true you are.

An illness of the mind and heart can only be treated with the appropriate medicine. If the wrong medicine is used, then all is lost.

Lack of achievement is not scary as one grows up. What is scary is losing direction and the ability to find oneself again.

Simple words are worth more after thought; simple things can be done to perfection. We often ignore the charm of simplicity on

our quest for complex perfection.

While holding on to attachment, it is difficult to accept kind words. Without wisdom in the heart, it is difficult to "let go".

Continuation of life lies in action, not passiveness.

There is one feeling, which is not loving and being together forever, but an affection between people. Without the affinity for marriage, this affection is the best choice.

The best words are no words. As long as two hearts know each other, words are redundant.

True happiness in life lies in giving not receiving. When you find the value of your life through selfless giving, you enjoy the happiness that is beyond others' imagination.

Those who accompany you in your work and life are the ones with true love in their hearts. Value such people; otherwise, once lost, you will never get them back.

A silent warmth is the parents' love to the children. If everyone can spread this warmth to every corner of the world, then the disasters in this world will cease quietly.

Slacking is a slow-releasing poison. It is already too late when you realize it.

Be the best you today regardless of what happened yesterday. This is the true meaning of life.

Valuing fame and gain will bring pain; Being indifferent to them will free you.

True beauty is not skin-deep. Kindness, modesty, and altruism bring true beauty.

Disappointments abound in our lives. During the glorious time, it feels like high noon with shining sun. When the sun sets, however, the last ray will subsequently disappear. Knowing this, we will be able to enjoy untroubled years of old age and realize that the beauty of life is in the state of no gains and no losses.

No need to invite everyone into your life. Life is after all a lone cultivation. Nevertheless, those who have entered your life, though they may not be the most suitable for now, they are important for certain phase of your life. Because of their existence, your life becomes full. None of the glories and none of the beautiful moments will last forever. Let's move on! Do not indulge yourself in the dreams of desire. No matter who you are with, all journeys are meant to be alone. Everyone and everything along the journey are means to cultivation.

Those with dreams may not reach the other shore after trying, but at least they get out of what is confining them. Those without any dream, will be buried in the dust and sand of time.

What is scary is not being poor economically, but in the heart. Such people do not see other's kindness as they pay attention only to their gains and losses. They are like a warm fire when they need your help, but become hard ice when you need them.

Sometime words are untrue; truth needs to be experienced first-hand.

Some say that the only person who can accompany you forever is yourself. In fact, those who truly love you are accompanying you every second with their hearts.

Thinking within a confined view, one pays attention only to losses and gains. If you can think beyond confinement, you will see a much broader world.

Keeping accompany is a way to show love. This kind of love, though silent, is pure.

Life goes on without high social status, but not without personal warmth. Perhaps you enjoy being low-key and do not seek out status. So long as you keep a grateful heart and pass on love and smiles, your warmth will gradually elevate your status.

Best metal comes from fire; beautiful lotus flowers grow out of mud. The fire brings out the brightness of the metal; the mud nurtures the purity of the lotus. Such is the rule of affinity.

The rich do not flaunt; the talented do not show off; and the capable do not brag. Those who are lacking in self-confidence and enjoy superficiality, on the contrary, like to elevate themselves through others' fame, wealth and abilities.

If a lotus flower complains about the dirty mud diminishing its beautify, the flower is not truly beautiful. If one constantly complains about one's family and job, then they will lose the entire world.

The experiences of the unknown may not be true, but it is surely a start to get to know the world.

Zhuangzi believed that a true free person is someone who is not controlled by their desires, who can adapt to changes, who is not tempted by fame and material gains, and who does not lose their true nature. Like a butterfly, such a s person, free from the various "status" put on people by the society, is truly beautiful and free.

Having a dream is not scary; what is scary is living in a dream and not being able to get out of it.

Luck and fortune are cultivated, not requested.

Anything that is gained through hypocrisy and lies will eventually be destroyed by righteousness and truth.

An old object, as long as it can be passed down from generation to generation, proves its unique value regardless of its authenticity. If you regard something as the best in your heart, then why bother with and be troubled by its authenticity.

Do not be greedy for what you really like because this kind of affection will turn out to be the kind of test that will destroy your future and life if you fail.

Those who are truly happy live a life of "subtraction" instead of "addition." The more you subtract from the external complicated decorations and let the true nature show, the more peace you achieve.

Some people live for others to see; some for their inner selves. The true exterior is only obtained from the true inner self. Happiness is real; living for others to see if not. Do not lose the true happiness.

Like a castle in the air, an ideal that is never carried out, allows you to live in an imaginary world and prevents you from seeing the real one.

The universe does not exist for itself and as such it lasts forever.

第二章

修身养性篇 / Self-cultivation

人贵在有自知自明，做事才能更好地去发挥个体的强项和天赋。反之，不仅弥补不了自己存在的弱点，还达不到最佳的效果。

欲伤害别人的人，所伤到的首先是他（她）自己。

天下有百病不生之药方否？

那就是养心。

养心的最佳状态就是每天在自我反省时不感到愧疚，面对天地可以神色泰然。

有修养的人习惯把自己放得很低，尊重他人的成绩。

自卑傲慢的人往往把自己抬得很高，把别人贬得很低。

想了解一个人的涵养如何，不妨先观察对方能否做到怒不变容，穷不失节。

学会退一步成全别人不是懦弱，而是修养。

借助做善事的名义而不做善事，只知道满足私欲的人，最终会受到良心的谴责。

当你以后遇到任何困难都不再怨天尤人时，那你生命中的顺缘一定比逆缘多。

精、气、神是人生至宝，嗜好吸烟的人精气神都不会特别好！

因为吸烟走肺，肺以气为主。如果你的肺受了伤，气就不够用了，自然就没了精神。

当你不了解自己心性的本源时，不要急于去探究困惑的根源。

当你悟到心性的本源时，一切困惑皆因此而解。

每个人的心中都有一片净土，只要把烦恼、嫉妒、嗔恨、贪痴心去掉，本具的那片净土自然就呈现出来了。

宽恕别人其实是在成就自己。

因为你每次想起他人伤己之痛，厌恨之毒就会重新伤害自己一次。

如果不及时宽恕曾经伤害你的人，厌恨之心爆发时就会重创自己和他人。

自己的变化不在别人的言语中，而是写在自己脸上。

欲了解自身的变化，不妨静心对着镜子审视。试着善心微笑，那么，所有向善的信息都绽放在笑容里。

不要以为你有钱、有地位，就会一点儿痛苦都没有。

如果你不摆脱痛苦的本性，这种快乐不会永远存续。

痛苦的本性就像人生了疮，而不去碰它一样，虽然暂时没什么感觉，但只要创伤在，肿痛、溃烂的危险就潜伏着，痛苦就可能随之而来。

同理，你不知现在的所为的一切，都会成为未来痛苦之因，眼前还没有感受到罢了。

舍得有不舍只求得、小舍求小得、小舍求大得、大舍求小得、大舍求大得、大小都舍不求所得等六个层次，唯有做到最后一种境界才是大智慧、大慈悲。

内心有阴影的人去行善，不是真慈悲，而是掩饰自己良心的不安。

真正的慈悲首先是敢直面自己内心的阴影，以无分别的心先唤醒自己再帮助他人。

坏习气是恶之源，发现就要立即克服。

否则，将一步一步把你引到黑暗的边缘。届时，你懊悔晚矣！

如果小的缺点不及时改正，大的节操随时会被葬送。

追求善的目的不仅为了他人还为了让自己能够回归宁静、光明、智慧的本心，做事永远先人后己。

做好事不是为了给别人看的，更不能为了名利而做好事。

心中有善，处处友善；心中有爱，时时友爱。

管住心，就能改变自身过往不良的习气。阳光辐照内心，才能找回真实的自己。

在没有见到自性前，请时刻观照好自己的六根，尤其是眼根和耳根。

只有找到了内在的自性，看图画才不会只停留在技法上，听音乐也不会只沉浸在旋律上。

判断一个人最真实的修养程度，不仅看他如何与熟人相处，还要观察他如何对待陌生人。

人的大气不是与生俱来的，而是在正能量的生活、工作环境中慢慢培养出来的。

大气是你的心，把心养好，就孕养了大气！

真正困扰你的一定是自己，而非他人。

如果能以一颗平常心去面对生活，就会祛除心中杂念，享受自在安宁的人生。对于圣人的心境，庄子如下阐释“至人之用心若镜，不将不迎，应而不藏，故能胜物而不伤”。

闲时不谈他人功过是非，行走坐卧检点自身不足，实乃修身养性之根本。

在修行中做事，在做事中修行。

睁开眼睛看别人都是优点，闭上眼睛观自己，扬长补短。

心善，做利他之事虽小也是大善。心不善，表面上做的善事再大，也背离善的本义。

你若每天看见他人的过失和是非，请立即自我反省，察省自身存在的问题。因为，你为他人缺点所恼时，实为被自身缺点纠缠。他人的过失亦即你的过失，关注他人的缺点，其实是给自己种下烦恼的种子。

世上没有永远的快乐，也没有永恒的痛苦。

不要总想着去改变别人，而要学会改变自己。

人对信仰的追求是为了让自己的内心有所归宿不再流浪，让精神世界有寄托而不再迷茫，让内心变得有爱心而不再自私，让人在所能及的能力范围内去帮助更多需要帮助的人。

如果有人把信仰变成了迷信，信仰即化为偏执！

没有经历过的事物永远是新鲜的，没有去过的地方永远是美妙的。

当你从幼稚走向成熟、从青年走到老年时才会恍然发现，这个世界其实是大同小异，美与丑、好与坏、真与假只是自己内心曾有过的分别。

不要刻意关注对方的热情是否真诚，毕竟热情要比冷漠好。

如果冷漠的人能坚持把伪热情带给别人，时间长了假热情也会变成真热情。

洗澡能清洗身体的污垢和疲惫，

心灵也需要用善的知识来洗涤负面情绪。

治病先治本，养生先养心。度人者先度己，修行者先修心。

生命的价值不在于你活着的时候为自己创造了多少财富，更在于你为世界及他人带来多少利益。

参与公益，既可以出钱，也可以出力或心。

在生活中存好心、说好话、做好事、做好人就是在参与公益，真实无漏。

行善不需要条件，参与公益慈善活动不必等到退休。

只要你做人做事多为别人着想，无论在世界哪个角落里都可以传递大爱。

每天在镜子前化妆、打扮、整理衣装的人不计其数，但能经常站在心灵的明镜子前反观检省自己言行、发心或三观的人并不多。

古代有“官无二业、事不并济”之说。

意思是只要你从事公务员的工作，要专心工作，既不能兼职其他职业，也不可将许多事业混淆在一起进行。如果一心二用，一定做不好本职工作。

深交后的陌生、认真后的痛苦、信任后的利用、温柔后的冷漠、朋友间的误解，其实并不可怕。因为这些现象都是心胸不够宽阔、做事为自己想得多，以为别人做得少所致。

只要做人光明磊落，做事心底无私，以上的现象就不易发生。

倘若你平时的一言一行都是为了别人，那根本就不必寻求自利，利他就是利己。

水无野心而清静，冰因谦虚而透明。

如果能学习水的清静和冰的虚心，那你就能变得像冰和水一样纯洁清通。

无论是平民百姓还是社会精英，下岗工人还是成功人士，我们都应该培植爱心、提升境界，这是整个生命链条中最重要的事情。

当我们的心灵提升至富有慈悲心、遍布智慧的境地，才能让周围的一切都变得完美圆融、和谐美善。

对于生命的价值，每个人都会持有不同的观点，但首先不是体现在你为了温饱而苟且一生，也非为了珍惜自己的生命而自利一生。

最重要的是在从你记事到老去的过程中，为其他生命无私奉献过多少。

这！就是生命崇高的价值。

生活中，如果不能改变自私自利的观念，就无法做到善待别人。

从点滴培养自己无私的爱心，即可焕发无限的正能量。因为无私利他的过程，会形成巨大的能量场。

每人只有一颗心，一旦滋生起贪心，你身体的健康就会失去平衡。

如果心里充满了爱，生活中自然增添无限乐趣，幸福将时常伴随你左右。

每一次雾霾的出现都是人心最真实的对境，只有历经人生的雾霾，你心中的阳光才会拨开迷雾照亮世界。

不要埋怨空中的雾霾影响了你的健康，而要反思自己私欲是否过重，你的生活方式是否绿色环保？

种瓜得瓜，种豆得豆。

播种一份爱心，收获一份福田。传递大爱阳光，享受幸福人生。

喝酒勿贪杯，贪杯失态还伤己。

醉酒之后所表现出来的言行，都是此人修养和习性的真实展现。

欲壑难填，欲望系烦恼之源，如何对抗？

用无求对治欲望，让施舍对治贪心，去奢降欲，你就不会患得患失而徒增烦恼。

真正的美是内心的淡定和从容，极致炫耀或傲慢无理是美的杀手。

人生最有价值的节省应该是对时间的有效控制。

请打开自己所有的感官，来认识外部世界。请畅通自己所有的知觉，来探究内心空间。

在没有偏私的大爱里，洋溢正气的心定能遇见真诚或真爱！

常怀克己之心，常闭是非之口。

幸福自然日增，烦恼必然日减！

性格即命运。

决定自己命运的关键就是改变我们的心。

心的格局改变了，性格改善了，自己的世界也就改观了！

世间所有公认的好东西都供不应求，只有发端于自己内心的幸福感不会被别人抢夺失去，坐拥这种创造幸福的能力可以使你收获源源不断的幸福。

人生每一件事的发生都不多余，都是为了自我修炼的提升，所以不必计较得失！

那颗永远不变的善心能改变我们的形象、命运，改变生活的磁场，从我们个人做起，完善自身、立足自身，最终实现中华民族的伟大复兴。

误会是一个人的认知错觉。

消解误会是自我审视与反省的过程。

感谢误会让你历练、成熟，打开胸怀！

积习不改，名医无策。内心不净，求佛无果。

从不曾醉心于寂寞，却沉溺孤独难以自拔。

孤独会成瘾，你不战胜它，它便吞噬你，只有懂得让心灵释放和休养的人才能驾驭孤独，并能适度享受孤独，从而走出幽暗奔向真正的自由，放飞自我！

欲望像一条无限长的锁链，一环接连一环，环环相扣，把臣服于它的人套牢，不加控制的欲望最终将变成锁住青春和人生的枷锁。

笑对春花秋月，淡看阴晴圆缺，花自开，水自流，心情澄明，不惹闲愁。

做人必先修身。

对内要做到心性正直，对外要做到举止优雅、仪容端正。

贪心乃人性之大忌，大贪大失，小贪小失。在哪儿贪，必在哪儿栽倒。

不信你回头看看，那些曾经在财、色、名、利，吃、喝、玩、乐上贪图享受、靡烂一时者最后的结局，一切豁然明了。

你还贪啥？

华而不实的虚名犹如过眼烟云，瞬间即逝。

那些羡慕、贪图一时虚名的人，反而会给自己带来实实在在的祸患及烦恼。

我喜欢你原本纯真的心地，以及如水般漾开的清雅。

所以请不要猜测或为讨我的欢喜，更无须为我将自己改造成连你都陌生的雕像！

一个人可以用爱得到全世界，也可以因恨失去所有。

常常喜欢把自己封闭起来的人，不论你出于何故离群索居，不关注外界和他人，只关注“小我”的内心，即使你比别人更仁慈、更高尚，但是对于大众来说你的价值都无法真正得以体现。其实真正的“桃花源”存在于平静忘我的心境中。

心中聚集的负能量就像天空的乌云一样，会越积越多，如果不及时清空分流，我们的心灵将不堪重负。

扫尽阴霾的最好办法就是打开心胸，让阳光照射进来！

人生的路没有尽头，累了，请停下来歇一歇！

也许，这时你才发现路边的风景其实很精彩。

生活中常听到的那些不顺耳的话，遇到的那些不顺心的事，是进德修行的砥石。

如果能用乐观积极的心态把听到的话儿句句都变顺耳，遇到的事儿件件都变顺心，这才是大智慧。

宁做方向对头的乌龟，不做方向错误的兔子。

宁做无私利他的阳光，不做祸国殃民的败类。

所有的心灵鸡汤都来自人们在不同时期、不同年龄阶段对生活的感悟，而非教化。

心里有了性欲的贪婪，千万不要想着去满足，因为行为上一旦满足，就好比喝了有毒的冰水，会越喝越渴。

如想解毒，就治标先治本，用坦荡纯净的正能量去对治性欲的嗔毒。

智慧的人习惯从自己身上发现问题，愚痴的人喜欢从他人身上寻找弊病。

要想自己脱离愚痴，就要养成经常观察自己内心变化、念头善恶的好习惯。这个好习惯的名字叫“内观”。

当心中充满爱时，黑暗处都会有光芒涌入。

人生的修行重在于行，而不在于言。

做任何事情都应该脚踏实地，不能只说动听浮华的话而没有实际行动。

福祸、苦乐如影随形。

心存善念，福乐同行。心生恶念，自招祸苦。

人们通常乐于接受怎样的热情或倾向于回应怎样的热情？

源于爱而没有侵犯性的真诚流露，更易被接受和传递，源于爱的热情无需伪装和矫饰，就这样自然而然地在人与人之间融汇和流淌！

幸福没有绝对定义也没有标准答案。

虽然快乐与幸福不能等量齐观，但是懂得从生活点滴中创造快乐的人更易获得幸福，反之，总是因计较小事而不快乐的人就缺乏发现幸福的眼睛和心灵。

幸福不需大而全，它真的可以小而美。

每个有信仰的人都会认为自己的信仰是最好的、至高无上的。

但千万不要因为过于执着自己的信仰，却给家人、给朋友带去烦恼。

因为信仰本身是帮助信仰者开启智慧、解除烦恼，而不是用你的信仰去衡量和要求别人。

在心灵成长这条人迹罕至的路上，打开心灵之锁的钥匙始终握在自己手里。

很多时候，心灵成长、成熟所需要的，不仅限于建议、教导、方法等，其实最能滋养心灵的是爱与阳光。

幸福在哪里？

它在别处吗？

其实你不必千里追寻，它一直就在你身边如影随形。

如果此刻你未感觉到心动的幸福，那么请你努力行动并真诚期许，幸福从未走远，它就站在能听得见你呼唤的不远处等你爱的回应。

越是弘扬正能量，正气就越多，越是倾诉传递负面情绪，负能量就越大。

当你特别无助的时候，只有放弃执着、坦然面对才有可能改变或接受事情的结局。

做人不能太自私，自私之人最终的结局是烦恼不断、抑郁而终。要想提高精神格局，就要学会无私利他。自私与无私之间的差距就是一个人的修养。

不怕被别人迷失，就怕迷失自我。心如莲花则可超然平淡，无分别心不失本我。

长期坚持行善的人身上会散发出特殊的香味，除此，其他人的身上都具有金木水火土所对应的气味。

夏天多出汗利于排毒，冬天少出汗利于养生。无论什么时候，掌握并遵循自然规律去生活，心无烦恼，百病不生。

心怀多少爱，做人就有多阳光。只关爱自己的人，对他人常常冷漠。

好色伤身，可还是有很多人就喜欢吃刀尖上的蜂蜜。这不是自控力差，而是没有自控力。

开心与不开心都是自己的事，千万不要因为不开心而影响其他人的情绪。没有谁应该为你的不开心去买单。

不要为了虚荣而掩饰真实，那样只会徒增烦恼。

走遍天下，最终还得回到原点。风光一生，也难免败走麦城。先认清自己，才有可能看清世间万物。

不中则不正。中则正，即为中正。

心不静则生火，阳火伤人，阴火伤己。心平则气和，气和则性柔，性柔则无火可发。脾气自然不会冲肝而伤人伤己。

道在人心，如水在地。虽高原平地，了不见水。苟穴土而求之，无不得者。

自夸难成，挑人伤己。顺势而为，道法自然。

天命生成的叫做性，顺着性发展的叫作道，依着道去休养叫做教。

世间万物皆有天命，但天命不可能永远不变。人如能行善道就能得到天命，不行善道将失去天命。

人的不良习气如杂草般难以根除，唯有多播善种，福田才会瓜果飘香。

内心空寂澄明时，才能发现繁星中最亮的一颗。它正是与你相对应的星星。

若能端正己身做人行事，周围的人与事物也会端正地亲近你。面对荣辱得失不动心的人，若非大富必定大贵。

妄心不除，真道难得。悟求真道，即不执不争，万念归一。

当不再为取舍、得失而烦恼，说明你正接近于道。常人脱离不了生与死、好与坏、对与错、真与假、正与反的阴阳五行之变。

爱在心里，无需远求。

人之气，吹则凉，呵则温。多思气乱，多言气散。

无论远还是近，都是心里的距离。

何谓大小？明明德于天下为大，于一身为小。

无论前面风景如何，路还得自己走。索性带着好心情行走，不因客观条件为自己徒增烦恼。

真心做到不计较，这是拔除所有病根的神药。

所有在生命里出现过的人，缘尽时，都会离你而去，无论怎样努力都无济于事。若不想缘尽时后悔悲伤，那就珍惜当下和身边人团聚的欢乐时光吧！

智慧的源泉，来自于宁静的内心。

仁义是心灵的声音，心灵的血脉。

在小鸟儿的眼里，虫儿胜过宝石。在君子的眼里，真诚、信誉、仁义、情谊高于一切。

养生的关键是清心寡欲，常怀善心。如刻意追求结果反而成了自私自利。

定期清理家里那些不需要的物品，会备感净洁。如能时不时清理一下精神上的垃圾，便会神清气爽。

外表的美丽需要丰富的内涵滋养，而不是浓

妆艳抹去画蛇添足。穿衣戴帽、梳妆打扮要结合年龄、季节、场合而搭配，如果偏离了度就容易物极必反。

女人葆有青春容貌的最佳方法是放下虚荣，谦虚做人；去掉傲慢，增加内涵；布施微笑，收获祝福。

心灵的美既可以保鲜，还可以保值。外表的美犹如昙花一现，再也无法回到昨天。

要想花开富贵，就要学会用德行去培育自己的福报。

千变万化都是心的变化，所以不要执着变化。心之外本来什么都没有，何来的千变万化？如果你静观本心，即可发现根本没有变，只有执。

无私增智慧，利他增福报。

真实的你喜欢安静，虚伪的你多是外向。真正的本我不爱伪饰，不擅长表演，只有自欺欺人者才习惯伪装。

放下真知灼见，放下曾经的辉煌，放下虚荣前的傲慢，看看裸露的肌肤上还有什么是你最值得自豪的？不是聪明才智，也不是智慧与学识，而是真实的本心。

心乱看什么都是逆境，心静看什么都是顺缘。

心有多净，世界就有多静。

你的美是天地父母给予的，无需在意他人的评价。你的爱是大公无私的，也无须在意他人的眼光。做一个善良、美丽、有爱心的人不是为了展示给别人看，而是做给天地父母看，是清净爱心的守护。

站在身体之外灵魂之上问你是谁？当你问清楚了你是谁时，你自然就成了你。你同时也明白了如何独处！

一物不能有二名，说触就不应说身，说身就不应说触。所以说“即触非身，即身非触。”

内心善良的人无论穿什么衣服都会让人干净清爽，而不善者无论如何穿戴，给人的气场都不舒服。

好斗伤肝，好色伤肾，好吃伤胃。人若能知己之好，便可远离疾病。

家族有多厚的德行，就有多好的运气。祖上或个人有多高的德行，就能享受多厚的福报。

人可以不够完美，但一定要不断地完善自性。

心同即道同，道泰则心泰。

分享的正能量越多，身上正能量的磁场就越强。传递的负能量越多，身心里的垃圾就会越积越满。

你有发表意见的权利，但必须深入调查了解才有真知灼见。否则，只能做一个依附别人发声的小丑。如果想让别人尊重并认可你，就要做个既能高瞻远瞩，又能深入一线无私利他的人。

无私则无欲，无欲则无念。无念则心定，心定则慧光自生。

对人有多傲慢，身体产生的负能量就有多少。对人有多尊重，就会产生多少正能量。

烦而不语，喜而不欢，藏而不露，高而不争乃修心养性之根本。

能看清自己，才能看清别人。

道理在说给别人听的同时，也是说给自己听的。如果能把道理和行为有效结合起来去修正自己，就是言行一致，无限增益。

诸事勿贪多，欲望越大、贪求越多，反作用力就越大。

做任何事情都要有一颗平常心，经常患得患失很容易滋生不必要的烦恼。

当想做的事一直迟迟不能推进时，说明福报和德性不足以承载这件事。只要净其心，观其欲，去其垢，就能点亮心中的希望之光。

真正的清净在于内心，无论外界环境怎么改变，内心的清净都不会变。

内心美，外面的世界才会更丰盈精彩。

情绪的剧烈变化会影响身心，导致阴阳的失衡，使体内的气血无法进行正常的运转，引起气血功能紊乱。

真实的自我是平静的、祥和的、没有任何造作的。若脱离了真实的自己，就远离了道，最终成为一个自己都不了解的人。

当心生恐惧不安时，请先自问因何事而不安，所有不安的因素来自于内心负面情绪的积累。

能战胜你的不是别人，更不是艰难困苦，而是内心的另一自己。

只有安住本心，才能了知万物发展的规律。若能看清自己的本心，就接近于道了。

人在一天中会产生不计其数的念头，只有让善念持久、稳定、有力，才能清静快乐。

不要看不起别人，也不可看不起自己。唯以敬畏看人看己，才会发现别人和自身被掩盖的优点。

不懂感动就不会感恩，容易被感动的人都是内心柔软善良，懂得感恩之人。

真正的修行是脚踏实地、通达圆融、表里如一，而非口是心非，夸夸其谈。

忘记自己是谁，才能真正找到无我无味的体感。

看破方明苦非真苦，乐非真乐。放下即能体悟苦即是苦，乐即是乐，皆在当下。

生活中，总会有无意识地伤害到别人而不自知的时候。虽不能说明自身存在问题，但某些习气需要及时反省。

心安则“天下”无事，心不安则事事不顺。若想求心安，就要常想他人所想，急他人所急。

内心干净，言行才会让人舒服。

人生最大的痛苦，莫过于欲壑难填。心所贪爱，不得其物。意在所谋，不遂其愿。两者不能称意，自苦于心。

真正的涵养不是自吹自擂的表演，而是从始至终表里如一的善行。

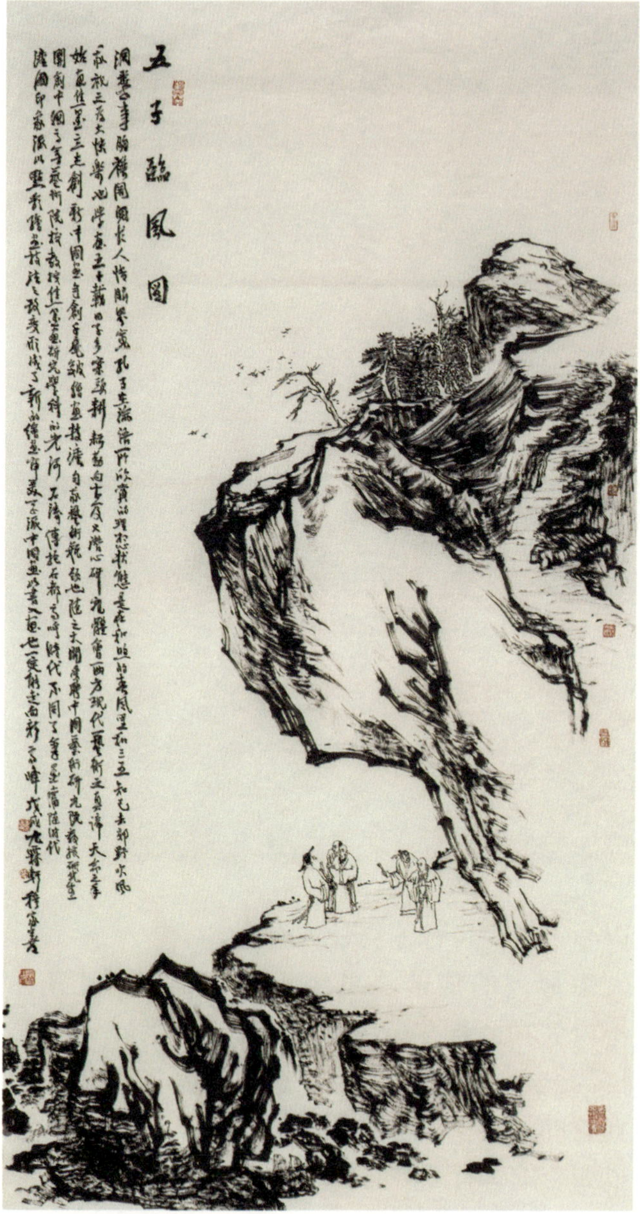
五子臨風圖

当日食、月食出现在大地上空时，请勿久视。因为，久视日食和月食会影响身体的磁场和运气。

心性成熟，定力十足的人不惧外界的任何干扰，反之则易受外界的影响而心生烦恼。

有脾气很正常，但发脾气也要适可而止，学会自我控制。否则，总有一天会为自己乱发脾气的行为买单。

把身上的贪嗔痴习气扫清，就能降伏其心。行住坐卧，动静闲忙，留得自在。

不要用真心对骗子，因为骗子不但不会被感化，骗了你还会说你傻。一旦发现有人不值得你用真心去对待，就趁早远离，以免白白浪费你时间和精力。

无论环境怎么变，心要守好，念不要动。如此方能心念如初，不为烦恼所牵。

养生之道，无过一静。老子清净，庄子逍遥。人唯清净而后能逍遥，逍遥则长寿也。

真正的智者不用经验和我执去判断事物的真伪，而是于心静处观无我。

人要活出自己的真实，无须为迎合他人的笑脸而改变自己的真性情。因为，真实的你一旦为他人改变就失去了本性。

坏习惯犹如麻痹人神经的毒药，一日不戒将中毒愈深。

人之祸福皆随心而起，心生善念则福气盈门，反之灾祸频频。

暖言可救人，恶语会伤人。习惯口吐莲花的人五官会越长越美，反之会影响自己的形象与运势。

傲慢则会让人无礼，无礼则会让人生厌。与其让人生厌不如谦虚做人，低调做事。这，才符合中庸之道。

命由己造，相由心生，世间万物皆是化相，心不动，万物皆不动，心不变，万物皆不变。

清净的身心如皎月高悬，看似孤寂，然内在的丰盈自心最知晓。

心正则身正，身正则正气生，唯正气可以滋养心性。

能长寿的不一定是每天锻炼身体的人，但性格开朗，与人为善、勤于思考、生活有规律的人一定会长寿。

心有敬畏则远离灾祸，心无敬畏则自找苦吃、烦恼不断。

心中有道，则万物通达。

喜欢去改变别人的人经常会因无法改变别人而

烦恼，而喜欢改变自己的人则经常因自己小小的改进而开心。

低头不是无能，宽容不是软弱。笑着低下头，不仅是一种修养，更是一种格局。

习惯口吐莲花的人内心一定干净无比 ，而常以恶语伤人者内心多存不净，长而久之则伤人伤己。

不管是圣人还是君子，管好自己的嘴是基本修养，巧言令色的人向来为孔子所不齿，最重要的是——君子是要说真话的人，而真话往往不好听，所以更要慎言。

学会珍惜福自来，不懂珍惜福远去。

真正的自由不单是言行的自由，而是内心不被欲望所束缚。

人的正能量不仅可以养精蓄锐，还是养生的良药。负面情绪不仅会影响周围的人，还会伤及自己的身心。

心量多大，福报就有多宽广。

人有众过而不自悔，顿息其心。罪来赴身，如水归海，渐成深广。若人有过，自解知非，改恶行善，罪自消灭。如病得汗，渐有痊损耳。

不能真正了解自己内心的人，生命总会被外力所牵引。因为，心中没有丘壑，人生只能跟着欲望随风飘荡。

人心正，所遇到的人和事皆为正品。人心不正，则事事不正，处处都会耽误自己，且渐行渐远离正道。

人生是一本书，封面是父母给的，内容由自己撰写。厚度不完全由本人决定，但精彩却由自己创造。

若想自己自在，首先要让身边的人得自在。

智慧可以让我们明辨是非，无知，则是一种恶。无知的人在事情发生之前，总是不相信恶行会出现自身，而智慧则让人谦虚而谨慎。

无知的人若是拒绝学习，他永远也无法对自己与他人有一个正确的认识，这种傲慢会将无知带入歧路，引入深渊。

永远保持谦虚的态度，不间断自我学习，也是一种行善。只有学习，才可以让我们摆脱无知，增加有意识的善，减少无意识的恶。

“禅”是什么？它什么都不是又什么都是！它不是形态，它是一种状态，是借着自然界的事物来思考的一种状态。

禅是海水，苦涩咸腥；禅是河水，无色无味；禅是湖泊，明如镜，浑如泽。如果要禅说风，就必须借助于植物，从植物摆动的形态联想到风的存在，看不见风却感知风的走向。

禅是什么？古人云：如人饮水，冷暖自知！

修身是中国人处世哲学中的第一步，而修身的第一步就是克制。人需要有一颗检讨自己的心，才能克制约束自己的欲望；能够克制约束自己欲望，才能成就自己。

幸福桥

People should know their own limitations, so that they can make the best of their individual advantages and talents; otherwise they can neither make up for their weaknesses nor enhance their strengths.

Those who want to hurt others will first do themselves an injury.

Is there a recipe for all diseases in the world?

Of course, it is to cultivate your mind.

The best state of that is feeling no guilt during everyday self-reflection, and facing the world with self-possession.

Cultivated people are used to putting themselves at a very low status and look up to others.

But as for self-abased and arrogant people, the situation is always totally opposite.

In order to know a person's self-restraint, one should first observe whether he could control his temper and maintain his integrity in poverty.

It is cultivation rather than cowardice to learn to make a concession to help others succeed.

Those, who do good only by mouth and care about nothing but their own desires, will eventually be condemned by their conscience.

If you no longer complain about others when encountering any difficulty, you will enjoy a much smoother future.

Vigor is the most precious thing in life, but those who love smoking will not be vigorous.

Tobacco smoke goes through your lungs which controls the vital energy of your body. Thus, if your lungs get hurt, the energy there will be far from enough, and you will run out of vigor naturally.

If you do not understand the origin of your disposition, then you shouldn't rush to explore the source of confusion.

When you understand that origin, all your puzzles will be solved accordingly.

Everyone has a piccc of pure land in his heart, which will naturally show up as long as he removes his trouble, jealousy, hatred, and greed.

To forgive others is in effect to realize self-attainment.

Because every time you think of the pain caused by others, the poison of hatred will hurt you once again.

If you don't forgive those who hurt you in time, the outbreak of hatred will hurt both yourself and others.

Changes in a person are shown on the person's face, not by other people's comments.

To notice your changes, take a look in the mirror. Try to smile kindly at the mirror, and you will find everything that is kind is in that smile.

Do not think that there will be no pain at all as you have much money and a relatively high status.

If you don't get rid of the nature of pain, happiness will not last forever.

The nature of pain is like a sore on the body. Without touching it, people feel nothing for the moment, but as long as it is there, the risk of swelling and festering is hidden and the pain may follow.

In the same vein, you feel nothing now because you don't know all you do at present will bring about pain in the future.

There are six degrees of one's willingness to part with his possessions. Namely, no pay but all gains, a little pay for a few gains, a little pay for many gains, much pay for a few gains, much pay for many gains, and all pay for no gain. Among these, only the last one is of great wisdom, great compassion.

As for the people whose heart is covered with shadow, it is

not true mercy but only a mask for their guilt when they practice philanthropy.

True mercy, firstly, is to have the courage to face the dark side of their inner world, awakened with no discrimination and then help others.

Bad habits are the source of evil, and thus must be overcome immediately once found out.

Otherwise, it will lead you to the edge of the dark step by step. By then, it is too late to have regrets!

If you don't correct your inconspicuous shortcomings in time, the moral integrity will be ruined at any time.

The pursuit of the good is not only for others, but also for oneself to return to the quietness, brightness, and wisdom of the true heart, and put the interest of others above his own.

Doing good is for neither spectators nor fame and fortune. The good in heart should be done in any place, and the love in heart should be shown at any moment.

Control your heart, and you can overcome your past bad habits; fill it with sunlight, and you can find your true self.

Before meeting your true nature, please control your six roots of sensation, especially your eyes and ear.

Only after finding out your true nature, you will notice more than techniques or melody when appreciating pictures or listening to music.

The judgment of one's self-cultivation should be based on how he gets along with strangers as well as his acquaintances.

Magnanimity is not innate, but gradually cultivated in a positive life and working environment.

Magnanimity refers to your mind, and therefore the cultivation of mind will attribute to the formation of magnanimity.

What can trouble you must be yourself, not others.

If you can face life with a non-discriminating heart, you will banish distracting thoughts from your mind and enjoy the peace of life. Zhungzi described the mind and heart of a sage as follows: "The sage's mind is like a mirror, which reflects what comes to it, but does not keep what leaves. Because it neither seeks nor hides, it can win and does not get hurt."

Never gossip about merits and demerits of others at your leisure; examine yourself at any time. These are the true essence of self-cultivation.

Do your work and self-cultivation at the same time, and the two will benefit each other.

Open your eyes and see other people's advantages; close your eyes and examine yourself before playing up your strengths and making up for your weaknesses.

Small altruistic actions with good intentions are of much benevolence, while actions with bad intentions, no matter how big the scale of the charity is, deviate from the true meaning of kindness.

If you see others' demerits and faults every day, please reflect on yourself immediately because when you are troubled by other's faults is in fact when you are tangled in your own shortcomings. Demerits you see from others are exactly the ones you possess yourself. Paying attention to others' shortcomings is in effect planting the seed for your own vexation.

There is neither everlasting joy nor eternal pain.

Don't think about changing others all the time; learn to change yourself.

The pursuit of faith enables the mind to find a shelter, the inner world to have support, and the heart to be filled with love.

With this pursuit, people with the ability are willing to lend a hand to others who need help.

However, if someone turns his faith into superstition, then the faith becomes prejudice.

The things you never experience will always be fresh; the places you never visit will always be wonderful.

However, as you age and mature, you will suddenly realize that the world is in fact very much the same. Beautiful or ugly, good or bad, true or false, all are nothing more than the distinctions made by the mind in the past.

Do not deliberately examine whether other people's enthusiasm is sincere or not. After all, enthusiasm is better than indifference.

And if indifferent people can keep on bringing the faked passion to others, such passion will become real eventually.

Taking a bath can wash away dirt and fatigue.

The mind also needs to be cleansed by benevolence to eliminate the negative emotions.

To cure diseases, one needs to start from the root; to keep in good health, one needs to start from the heart; to get others out of trouble, one needs to start from himself, and cultivate himself from his mind.

The value of life is measured by how many benefits you have brought to others and the world rather than how much wealth you have created for yourself when you are alive.

To participate in public welfare, you can offer either money or efforts and love.

In daily life, it is also such a participation to keep mercy in mind, mouth, and actions.

Practicing philanthropy is unconditional. Therefore, if you want to participate in charitable activities, you don't have to wait until retirement.

As long as you always put others in mind, you can spread love to every corner of the world.

Countless people will make up and dress up in front of the mirror every day, but only a few would pay attention to their expressions or reflect on the value of their life.

In ancient times, a saying went that "officials had no other business and affairs should never be handled at one time."

It means that as long as you work as a civil servant, you have to concentrate on your work, and cannot hold other posts. Besides, you should not do multiple jobs at one time. If you do, you will not perform your duty well.

Strangeness after intimate association, pain after taking others to heart, being taken advantage of after trusting in them, indifference after treating each other with gentleness, and misunderstanding among friends, all of these, in fact, are not terrible because they are caused by narrow-mindedness and selfishness.

As long as you stay upright, honorable and selfless, they won't happen easily.

If your words and deeds are all for others, you simply don't have to seek interests for yourself as those for others are also for you.

With no ambition, water is peaceful and quiet; thanks to modesty, ice is transparent.

If you can learn the quietness of water and the modesty of ice, you can become as pure and clear as ice and water.

No matter who we are, ordinary people or social elites, laid-off workers or successful people, we are all supposed to cultivate compassion and refine our mind, which is the most important in our life.

Not until when we have both benevolence and wisdom can we make everything around us beautiful and harmonious.

As for the value of life, everyone holds a different point of view. But first of all, it is reflected neither in your muddle only to ensure you food and clothing, nor in your selfishness only to cherish your life.

The most important thing is how much dedication you have selflessly made to other people's life from your childhood to old age.

This is the lofty value of life.

If you cannot abandon your selfishness in daily life, you can never be kind to others.

Cultivate your selfless love little by little, and you can call forth infinite positive energy because the process of practicing altruism can create a huge energy field.

Everyone has only one heart. Once you become greedy, your health will be out of balance.

But if your heart is full of love, there will naturally be much more fun in your life, and happiness will always be with you.

Every appearance of haze is the true reflection of the mind. Only after experiencing the haze of life can the sunshine in your heart clear the fog away and light the world up.

Do not blame the haze in the air for affecting your health, but reflect on whether you have too many desires or your lifestyle is not eco-friendly.

As a man sows, so shall he reap.

Thus, sow the seeds of love, and you can harvest a field of happiness; transmit the sunshine of love, and you can enjoy a happy life.

Don't indulge in excessively drinking, which usually leads to an embarrassing gaffe and does harm to your health.

Also, what you say and do when you are drunk is the true expression of your cultivation and character.

Avarice is the source of worries and knows no bounds. Then how to fight against it?

Desire for nothing, give alms, and abandon luxury, and you

will not unnecessarily get into trouble because of worrying about personal gains and losses.

The real beauty is inner calm instead of flaunt or arrogance which kills all beauty.

The most valuable savings in life should be the effective control of time.

Please mobilize all your sensory organs to learn the outer

world, and stimulate all your feelings to know the inner world.

Surrounded by unbiased love, the heart full of righteousness will meet true sincerity and love!

Restrain yourself and never gossip about others.

Then you will naturally become happier and less worried.

Character means fate.

The key to determining our fate is making changes to our minds.

With minds changed and characters improved, we can therefore change our inner world.

The supply of generally recognized good things falls short of demand. Only the happiness originating from your heart can't be

robbed by others. And the possession of this ability enables you to keep receiving happiness without end.

Everything happening in life is not redundant but meaningful for the self-cultivation. Thus, it brings nothing but harm to keep account of gains and losses.

The eternal benevolence can change our images, destinies and energy field. We all improve ourselves, starting from ourselves and finally realizing the great rejuvenation of the Chinese nation.

Misunderstanding is one's cognitive illusion.

Clearing the air is the process of self-examination and reflection.

Thanks to misunderstanding, you have got lots of experiences that have made you mature and broadened your mind.

If ingrained habits are not corrected, even prestigious doctors won't know what to do with them. If the heart is not pure, even the Buddha won't give an answer when prayed to.

You might have never been engrossed in loneliness but too obsessed with solitude to extricate yourself from it.

Solitude can be an addiction. If you do not overcome it, it will devour you. Only those who know how to free their mind can manage to enjoy it in moderation, and thus get out of the darkness, run towards real freedom, and let oneself soar!

Desire is like an infinitely long chain with interlocked rings, which entangles itself with those who surrender to it. If not controlled, the desire will eventually become a yoke of youth and life.

Smile at seasonal scenery and be indifferent to wax and wane. Like blooming flowers and flowing water, you can get rid of unnecessary worry as long as you keep your heart pure.

Life must start from self-cultivation.

Be a person of integrity with elegant manners and graceful appearance.

Greed is the taboo of human nature. The more you covet, the more you will lose; where there is a covetous thought there is a loss.

If you don't believe this, just look back at the endings of those who once indulged in wealth, lust, fame and gain, gluttony and pleasure-seeking. All is clear.

What are you greedy for then?

Flashy fame is as transient as fleeting clouds that disappear in a twinkling.

Those who admire and covet temporary reputation will bring themselves scourges and troubles.

I like your original innocent nature and the elegant appearance that is as fresh as flowing water.

So please do not guess my preference or please me; let alone transform yourself into a strange statue even you yourself can't recognize.

A person can get the whole world with his love, but can also lose it all due to hatred.

Those who prefer the life of a recluse and care about themselves rather than others and the outside world, for whatever reasons, cannot realize their values for the public, even if they are kinder or more noble than others. In fact, the real Land of Peach

Blossoms (meaning "paradise" in Chinese) exists in a calm and selfless mind.

Negative energy gathered in the heart is like dark clouds that will accumulate. If we fail to clear the clouds away in time, our hearts will be overwhelmed.

The best way to sweep such haze away is to open our minds and let sunshine in!

Life has no end. Thus stop to take a break if you get tired.

Perhaps at that time, you will find the scenery on the roadside is actually very magnificent.

The harsh words and unsatisfactory things in daily life are the whetstones of self-cultivation.

The great wisdom is to turn both into pleasing ones with the help of an optimistic and positive attitude.

The turtle that knows the right direction is preferable to the rabbit that runs in the wrong direction.

Likewise, selfless sunshine is infinitely better than the scum that causes grave harm to the state and the people.

All the so-called "chicken soups for the soul," or inspirational words, are not indoctrination but perceptions people draw from their life at different times and ages.

Don't consider meeting your sexual desires; otherwise you will be thirstier as if you have drunk toxic ice water.

To detoxify yourself, you should fight against the poison of sexual desires with positive energy as the saying goes that "cure for

a disease goes before that for symptoms".

The wise are used to finding problems from themselves, while the ignorant like to look for shortcomings from others.

To get rid of ignorance, you are expected to develop a habit of constantly observing your inner changes and thoughts, namely "introspection".

With a heart full of love, even the dark crannies will be filled with sunshine.

Self-cultivation mainly focuses on your deeds rather than your words.

You are supposed to be down-to-earth no matter what business you are handling. It never works to say high-sounding words without practical actions.

Weal and woe go hand in hand as enjoyment and suffering do.

Keep mercy in mind, and you will be accompanied by weal and enjoyment; have vice in mind, and you will spell woe and suffering.

What kind of enthusiasm are people usually willing to accept or respond to?

The inoffensive enthusiasm originating from love is received and passed on more easily because it needs no disguise or pretense.

Happiness has no absolute definition or standard answer.

Although joy doesn't equate to happiness, those who know how to create joy in daily life are easier to obtain happiness. On the contrary, those who fuss about trifles and therefore have little joy cannot find their happiness with their eyes and heart.

Happiness doesn't have to be big and complete; instead, it really can be small and beautiful.

Every believer thinks his faith is the best and supreme.

But do not bother your family members and friends with it.

Because faith is not to evaluate others and make requirements for them, but to enlighten its believers and relieve their worry.

On the less traveled road of spiritual growth, the key to the soul is always held in your own hands.

In many cases, spiritual growth and maturation need more than advice, instruction and methods. In fact, the most mind-nourishing things are love and sunshine.

Where is happiness?

Is it really elsewhere?

In fact, you do not have to pursue it thousands of miles because it is always with you.

If you can't feel happiness right now, please make an effort and wish sincerely. Happiness has never gone far away. It is standing over there where it can hear you, and waiting for your response of love.

The more promotion of positive energy, the more positive "Qi" flows; the more talking and spreading of negative emotions, the stronger the negative energy.

When no one comes to your help, the only thing you could do is to let go of your attachment and face the music. Only by doing so can you change or accept the outcome.

One cannot be too selfish. A selfish person eventually ends up in a death of constant annoyance and depression. Altruism is the key to improve one's spiritual life. The distance between selfishness and altruism is simply one's cultivation.

What one should be fearful of is not being forgotten by others but losing oneself. With a heart as pure as the lotus flower and without any discrimination, one can stay calm under dull circumstances and not lose oneself.

Those who do good deeds consistently for a long period of time give out a special fragrance. The rest emit the smells corresponding to the five elements of metal, wood, water, fire and earth.

To sweat more in the summer detoxifies the body; to sweat less in the winter benefits one's health. Regardless when it is, live your life by following the natural way, no worries, no illness.

A sunny disposition is proportional to the love in the heart. Those who care only for themselves tend to be cold to others.

Lust damages health. However, many people would pursue lust as if eating honey on the blades of the knife. This is not weak in

self-control; this is not having any self-control.

Being happy or unhappy is one's own business. Please do not make other people's mood rotten because of your unhappiness. No one has the responsibility to pay for your unhappiness.

Do not conceal reality for vanity. Doing so can only bring vexation.

Travel all over the world, and one eventually returns to the

starting point. Being successful the entire life cannot avoid defeat. Knowing who you are first, you can then know what is in the world.

Uprightness comes from being in the middle. The middle way brings fairness and just.

A restless mind produces the element of "fire", The Yang fire hurts others; the Yin fire hurts oneself. A serene mind brings harmonious Qi. When the Qi is harmonious, then the temperament is gentle. With gentle temperament, there is no temper to lose and naturally the liver will not be harmed and avoids hurting others and oneself.

The Tao lies in our hearts and minds just like water flows on the ground. When no water can be seen in a plateau or plain, dig a hole to seek it out and you will find it.

Self-praise ends in vain; provoking others hurts oneself. Go with the flow as the Tao follows nature.

What heaven conferred is called the Nature; an accordance with that nature is called the path (Tao); the regulation of this path is called instruction.

Everything in this world has a heavenly nature, which will not stay unchanged forever. If one can practice the path of kindness, he will fulfill the heavenly nature. Otherwise, the heavenly nature will be lost.

Like weed, bad habits cannot be uprooted easily. By spreading good seeds, the field can be fruitful.

A serene heart will enable you to see the brightest star in the sky, which corresponds to you.

Conduct yourself in an upright manner, and you will find those around you draw close to you. Those who are not influenced by gains or losses will be destined to have either big fortune or big social status.

No truth can be obtained with wandering thoughts. To find the truth, one must neither attach nor seek. All thoughts return to one.

When you are not troubled by gains or losses, you are close to the Tao. Ordinary people are bound by life and death; good and bad; correct and wrong; true and false; positive and negative, all of which are phenomena of the changes of Yin Yang and the five elements.

Love is in the heart. No need to seek afar.

Qi of a person becomes cold when blew on; hot when cared for. Too many thoughts mess up the Qi; too many words scatter the Qi.

Far or near? It is the distance between two hearts.

What is big? What is small? Illustrating the illustrious virtues to the world is big; to oneself, small.

Regardless of what the scenery is awaiting you ahead, you still need to travel your path. Then why not travel with a happy mood and not bring unnecessary annoyance to yourself?

The magic pill to unroot any illness is truly being care-free.

Everyone that has been in your life will leave when the affinity no longer exists no matter how hard you try to keep them. To avoid the sadness then, why not value the present happy time when you are surrounded by people?

The origin of wisdom lies in the peaceful inner mind. Wisdom arises from meditative concentration.

Benevolence is the sound and the bloodline of the soul. A worm is worth more than a gem in the eyes of a bird. Sincerity, credibility, benevolence and friendship are above all in the eyes of a gentleman.

The key to cultivating health is having fewer desires and a kind heart. Deliberately seeking any rewards, on the contrary, becomes selfishness.

Getting rid of unwanted or unused items in the house regularly brings cleanliness to the home. If every now and then you can get rid of the garbage in your mind, you will feel refreshed right away.

Beauty of the appearance is nurtured by what lies inside, not through heavy make-ups. How to dress oneself depends on one's age, the season and the situation. Delineating from appropriateness can bring the opposite results.

The best way for a woman to stay youthful is letting go of vanity and conducting herself with modesty. By putting away arrogance, cultivating inside, and smiling, she will be blessed.

The beauty of the soul is long-lasting. The beauty of the appearance is short-lived, like a flash in the pan - it can never return to what it was yesterday.

To achieve wealth and social status, we must learn to use virtue to cultivate our own good fortune.

All changes trace to the changes of the heart. Therefore, there is no need to attach to any change. Nothing actual is there outside of the heart. Then, how can there be any changes? If you observe your true nature with tranquility, you will see there is no change but attachment.

Selflessness reaps wisdom; altruism increases good fortune.

The true self likes peace and quietness; the vain one pretends to be extraverted. The true self does not disguise nor perform. Only those self-deceivers are used to pretending.

Once the insight is put down, the past glory is gone, and the arrogance out of vanity is beyond, what is then worth your ultimate pride? It is not wisdom, nor knowledge; it is your true heart.

Everything is an adversity seen from a confused heart; all is advantageous seen from a peaceful heart.

The world is as quiet as the heart is pure.

Your beauty is endowed by heaven and earth and your parents; your love is selfless. Do not pay attention to others' evaluation. Being a kind, beautiful and loving person is not for showing to others. It is for heaven and earth and for the guarding of the pure and loving heart.

Ask yourself who you are from your soul. When you have figured out who you are, you naturally become you. At the same time, you also know how to be alone.

There cannot be two names for one thing. The act of "touching the body " - we cannot say it is touching; we cannot say it is the "body." The "body" is what is being touched; the "touching" is what is being sensed. So, the body is not the touching and the touching is not the body. The sensing and knowing does not belong to either.

A kind-hearted person makes others feel comfortable regardless of their attire. An unkind person makes others uncomfortable no matter what they wear.

Aggression hurts the liver, lusts the kidneys, and gluttony the stomach. If one can know oneself well, one can then be shielded from diseases.

Good fortune goes proportionally with the virtues of the family. One can enjoy fortune and blessings in proportion to their ancestors' or their own virtues.

A person cannot be perfect, but they can constantly perfect their true nature.

If the heart is the same, then the path chosen is the same. If the path is peaceful, then the heart is peaceful.

The more positive energy one shares, the stronger the positive energy magnetic field one creates. The more negative energy one passes, the fuller the mental and physical garbage one gathers.

You have the right to express your opinion; however, you cannot obtain true insight without deep research and understanding. Otherwise, you can only be a clown who depends on others for your own voice. To gain respect and recognition, you will need to be one who can not only look far beyond the horizon but also do everything you can to benefit others selflessly.

Selflessness leads to no desire; no desire leads to no thought.

No thought leads meditative concentration; meditative concentration brings forth wisdom.

The negative energy one produces is proportionally to their arrogance toward others. The positive energy to the respect.

Do not complain while being annoyed; do not exhibit jubilance while being happy; hide without revealing; reach high without competing. This is the essence of self-cultivation.

One cannot know others well until one knows oneself clearly.

The reasons and truth are not just for others; they are for us to listen to when we lecture others. If we can combine the truth and the action effectively to cultivate ourselves, we will achieve harmony between words and deeds, which brings endless benefits.

Greed for anything leads to more desires - the more the craving, the stronger the force leading to the opposite.

Do everything with an ordinary heart. Worrying about gains and losses constantly breeds unnecessary vexation easily.

When you cannot make any progress on something you want to do, it is an indication that your fortune and virtue is not enough to shoulder the responsibility of this deed. As long as you quiet your heart, observe your desires, get rid of your shortcomings, you will ignite the light of hope in your heart.

The real tranquility lies inside. No matter how the external environment changes, the internal tranquility stays the same.

With inner beauty at heart, the world outside will be more abundant and wonderful.

Dramatic changes in emotions lead to the imbalance of Yin and Yang, causing the internal Qi and blood circulation out of order which results in the dysfunction of Qi and blood.

The true self is calm, peaceful, and without any pretentiousness. If you break away from your true self, you will stay away from the Tao and eventually become a stranger to yourself.

When your heart is fearful and uneasy, please ask yourself why you are uneasy. All the unrest factors come from the accumulation of negative emotions in your heart.

It is not someone else who defeats you, let alone hardship, but the other self in your heart.

Only by true to your nature, can you understand the rules of development of all things. If you could see your true nature clearly, you are close to Tao.

A person produces countless thoughts everyday. Tranquility and happiness can be achieved only if one makes the kind thoughts last, steady and powerful.

Do not look down upon others; do not look down upon yourself either. Only by looking at oneself and others with awe can one discover the merits that are covered up by oneself and others.

One cannot be grateful until one knows what is being moved. Those who are easily moved are gentle and soft at heart and grateful. The true cultivation is down-to-earth, thorough and harmonious, consistent in appearance, not rhetoric.

Only by forgetting who you are can you truly find the sense of selflessness.

See through and you will understand suffering is not true suffering, and joy is not true joy. Let go and you will realize that suffering is suffering, and joy is joy, all in the moment.

In life, there are always times when we hurt others unintentionally and do not know it. Although it is not a statement that something is wrong with us, it is necessary to reflect on our habits timely.

If your heart is at peace, nothing is not at peace. If your heart is restless, everything you do can be troublesome. If you want peace of mind, you often must think about what others think and do what others do.

Only when you are pure inside can your words and deeds

make others feel comfortable.

The greatest pain in life is nothing other than insatiable greed. Not able to get what one loves and not able to fulfil a desire - both are unsatisfactory with suffering from the heart.

The true self-cultivation is not self-proclaimed performance, but a kind deed that is consistent in thought and action from beginning to end.

When either solar eclipse or lunar eclipse appears in the sky, please do not stare at it for too long because doing so will affect your body's magnetic field and your luck.

People with mature minds and concentration are not afraid of any interference from the outside world. Without, they are easily affected by the influence of the outside world and feel upset inside.

It is normal to have a temper, but tantum should be moderate. Learn self-control; if not, sooner or later one will pay for the action of losing temper without control.

Sweep away the residual habits resulting from greed, anger and ignorance, and you will subdue the heart and achieve total freedom in your daily life.

Do not treat swindlers with sincerity. They will not be moved,

and they will think you are stupid after cheating you. Once you discover that someone that does not deserve your sincerity, stay away in order not to waste your time and energy in vain.

No matter how the environment changes, as long as you keep a peaceful inside and not let wandering thoughts arise, you will keep to your original true heart and not be led by worries.

Nothing is better to cultivate health than being still. The Taoist masters of Laozi and Zhuangzi were tranquil and care free respectively. Care-free comes after tranquility; care-free leads to longevity.

A true wise person does not use their experience or ego-attachment to determine the authenticity of things. They determine by observing the "no self" in the quietness of the heart. We live to our true selves and do not need to change our true temperament to cater to the smiling faces of others, because once changed, you will lose the true you.

Bad habits are like a poison that numbs the nerves. As long as the habits are not gone, the poisoning will become more intense.

Weal and woe arise from the mind. Good thoughts lead to fortune; bad to disasters.

Warm words heal; harsh words hurt. Those who are used to giving compliments and saying kind words are more beautiful physically. Conversely, those who say the opposite will have their image and luck be negatively influenced.

Arrogance leads to rudeness. Rudeness makes others dislike you. It is better to be a humble person and act without self-effacing than being disliked by others. This is in accordance with the "Doctrine of the Mean".

Your fate is created by you; phenomenon arises from the mind. Everything in the universe is a reflection of the mind. If the mind is still, everything is still. If the mind does not change, everything does not change.

A pure and quiet body and mind is like the bright moon in the sky. Seeming lonely, but only your heart knows the richness inside.

The heart is rectified, then the body is upright. The body is upright, then the positive Qi and righteousness will rise. Only the positive Qi can nurture the temperament.

Those who live long might not be the ones who exercise every day. But those who are open, kind, inquisitive, and live their lives with regular routines are sure to live long.

Reverence in the heart keeps one away from disasters. Lack of reverence begs for trouble and constant vexation.

Tao in heart, everything is accessible.

Those who like to change others often become annoyed when they fail; those who like to change themselves are often happy because of any small improvement they make.

Yielding to others is not incompetent; tolerance is not weakness. Yielding with a smile is not only a sign of cultivation but also a state of broadminded.

Those who are used to giving compliments and saying kind words must be pure and clean inside. Those who hurt others with ill words often are dirty inside. As days go by, this will hurt both others and themselves.

Sage or gentlemen, being careful with words is a basic training. Those with insincere and ready words are disliked by Confucius. Most importantly, a gentleman is someone who tells truth, and truth is often unpleasant to the ears. Therefore, it is even more necessary to be careful with words.

Knowing to cherish brings luck in; Not knowing so drives blessings away.

True freedom is not just the freedom of words and actions; it is the freedom of the heart not being bound by desires.

A person's positive energy can not only preserve and restore energy but also serve as a good medicine for health. Negative emotions not only affect the people around you negatively, but also do harm to your mind and body.

How broad the heart is, how extensive the karmic rewards are.

No repentance for countless wrong doings, the goodness in the heart is thus extinguished. When sin comes, it will develop deeper and deeper, like water returning to the sea. Once committing wrong doing, if one can understand what is wrong and reforms from evil to good, then the sin is eliminated itself. This is similar to sweating during illness - the sweat brings recovery gradually.

For those who do not know their heart and mind truly, their lives are always drawn by external forces. Without principles and understanding inside, life can only follow desires and drift with the wind.

With a rectified heart and a balanced mind, all the people you meet and things you run into are genuine and wholesome. Conversely, you will run into trouble for everything, delay your growth everywhere, and stray away from the right path gradually.

Life is a book: the cover given by parents; the content written by ourselves. The thickness of the book is not solely determined by oneself, but the splendor is created so.

Want to feel at ease? Be sure to make people around you feel at ease first.

Wisdom enables us to discern right from wrong; ignorance is an evil. Ignorant people never believe that evil will occur before it happens. Wisdom makes people modest and cautious.

Refuse to learn, and the ignorant people will never obtain a correct understanding of themselves and others. This arrogance will bring ignorance onto a wrong path and leads it to the abyss.

Keeping a humble attitude forever and learning uninterruptedly is also a good deed. Only through learning can we get rid of ignorance, increase conscious good and decrease unconscious evil.

What is "Zen?" It is everything; it is nothing. It is not a form. It is a state - a thinking state through the objects in nature.

Zen is the water in the sea, bitter and salty; Zen is the water in the river, colorless and tasteless; Zen is a lake, bright as a mirror, simple as a luster. If we compare Zen to wind, we will need the help of plants. From the way plants swing in the wind, we imagine the existence of the wind. Although we cannot see the wind, we can feel the direction it travels.

What is Zen? As the ancient said, "It is like sipping water. Only the drinker knows if it is cold or warm."

Cultivating oneself is the first step in a Chinese person's philosophy of life, and the first step for self-cultivating lies in self-control. One must be able to self-criticize in order to control their desires. Not until the desires are controlled can one succeed.

第三章

为人处世篇 / Principles in Life

自己的事办不了可以找朋友帮忙，但自己都不喜欢做的事情一定不要让朋友做。这是交友之大忌讳。

做人拥有一副热心肠是好习惯，但不是对所有的求助都要答应。因为做一个热心肠的人，不仅要善于助人，也应该学会拒绝你没有能力做的事情。

不要以为有几个人表扬你，就认为所有人都认可你。认可你的人未必会当面夸你，而当面表扬你的人不一定真心认可你。

喜欢批评别人的人常认为自己很完美，实有不知，批评别人的行为就是人性中致命的缺点。

因听实话而受伤的人，是因为听习惯了假话。

生气的时候，请保持沉默，更不能做任何决定。因为人在生气的时候，所有的决定都是与理智背道而驰的。

嘴上应诺帮别人办事，但因能力不足或不行动的人不仅是心口不一，也是失信误人的人。因为这种行为，很可能让别人失去了一次成功的机会。

无私利，绝非嘴上说说，而是心甘情愿地去做且不求回报。如果你帮了他人得不到回报，心里就失落，开始埋怨，说明你有私心。否则，不会起烦恼。

能向你求字画的人，一定是欣赏你，并认为与你关系要好的人。如果你一定给自己的作品定价让对方出钱来买，就世俗化了，其实，所有懂得感恩的人都不会白要你的作品。

当有人要与你谈论他人隐私或是非时，一定当即给予制止。否则，此人转身之后，下一个非议的对象就是你。

与人交往难免会有意见不一致的时候，发生争辩也无可避免。但是，无论多么生气，都不能暴粗口或进行人身攻击，因为这些行为不仅伤人而且伤己。

请学会用温和的语气与人交流，不随意跟别人发脾气。在这个世界上，谁都不欠谁的。

做人如处处争先，必会迷入歧途，不利前行。如坚持以柔顺处世，时时先请他人前行，自己跟随其后，必能与君子同行，共见光明之境。

闲暇时，请不要热衷于打探人与人的是非和八卦。因为经常谈论这些事情百害无益。当你不再谈论别人的过失和隐私时，烦恼和无名火气自然消逝。

无论你珍藏多少书籍，都不足以证明你知识渊博。真正做学问的人，从不炫耀自己珍藏或者读过多少书。

习惯在举手之劳间给人一些帮助、布施一句好话、传递一个微笑的善者，德行就会日积增厚。如果能为而不为、不能为而为之，德行一定会有所损耗。

当你看到自己认为不合理的事情时，请先禁闭尊口。待你安静观察几分钟后，就会发现你所见的事情绝非刚才想的那样简单。

明明知道某事是错误的，为了保全自己的那点尊严和面子，找各种理由为错误开脱者，其实刻意保全的面子早已丢尽。

他人做事有弊端时，你可以正面剖析并给出改进意见，但不能揭人之短。揭人短处、伤人前途、坏人名誉的举动不是君子行为。

为了得到别人的恭敬而故意端着架子的人，所得到的恭敬不一定是真诚的；那些假装恭敬他的人，必然是想从他身上获取某些利益的人。

当别人不愿意讲自己的过往或者隐私时，请不要再纠缠不休地问下去。这样只会徒增他人烦恼。

不要为了利益而轻视道义，更不要贪恋利益而远

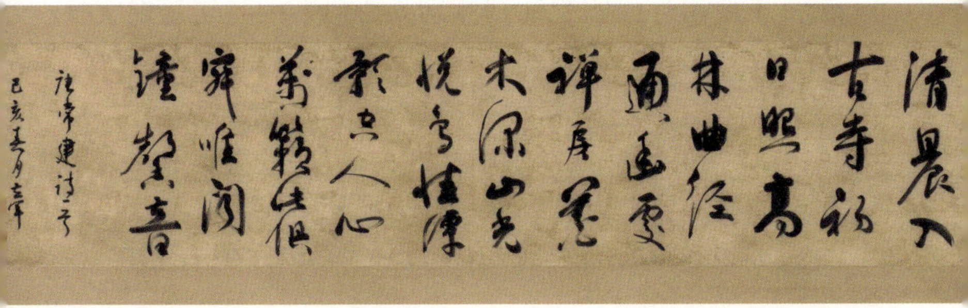

离信用。大家都能看见的利益，早已不是利益了。

人过于聪明就接近了愚蠢。愚蠢的人总是喜欢先计算个人利益，而有智慧的人会先考虑他人得失。

看破不说破，你每给对方一次体面的台阶，就多给自己一次进步的机会。

世间真有秘密可言？其实，当你知道某件事情的真相时，这事儿已经不再是秘密。

不要用自己的想法揣测别人心思，因为这是误会之源。

与人交往，要先想着自己能够让对方得到什么，而不是自己可以获得多少。得失都是成正比的，所以不要只想得到而不想失去。

如果心里常装着别人对自己的好，不想自己对别人的好，你的感恩之心就会增强，也不会因他人的一点点过失而指责抱怨。

有时候，如果坚持了你应该做却不想做的事情，会意外收获你想要的东西。

当你对某人做某事产生怀疑时，请不要再和某人继续做某事。因为自你怀疑心出现后，事情的走向已悄悄发生了变化。

请不要给别人制造捕风捉影和无中生有的言论，也许你不经意的玩笑会给对方带去巨大的伤害或恶果。

喜欢窥视或谈论别人隐私的人，或许其隐私已经众人皆知。

别人在生气或不理智时骂你的话，还是值得认真思考的，因为这些不中听的语言也许是此人对你最中肯的评价。

昼夜谋算别人的人，早晚会机关算尽，终把自己也算计进去。

做好事，身边所有的善者都会靠拢你。心存恶念，吉祥与善友都将远离你。

自学会说话至今，因负面言语产生的语言垃圾会一直积攒在你的身边。只有改变制造语言垃圾的习惯，并及时清理语言垃圾，你的能量空间和语言能量才会变得五彩斑斓。

两颗鸡蛋相碰，必定是先着力的鸡蛋先破裂。这个规律告诉世人，喜欢挑唆打架、发动战争的人终将以惨败告终。

每个人的优点和缺点都是并行而存。因此，与人相处既不能因喜悦而夸大对方的优点，也不要因烦恼而放大对方的缺点。

有舍才有得。正所谓大舍大得，小舍小得，不舍不得也。

国与国之间相交，人与人之间相处，如果都能持平和的态度去沟通，就会得以和平共处。

当善于挑拨离间的人给你灌输负面信息时，千万不要因为对方的言语挑拨激起盲目冲动，以至做出不理智的举动。因为，能管理好自己情绪的人才不会轻易被他人利用，也会远离过失。

宽恕别人就是善待自己，记恨别人则在惩罚自己。

承诺很重也很轻。牢记自己对别人的承诺，做到合乎礼节、认真实践，则重。忘记别人给自己的承诺，不求兑现、得失顺其自然，则轻。

我不懂我不说，你懂你请说。不怕不懂，就怕不懂装懂。

如果你习惯倾听别人的心声，你将会拥有天下最宝贵的财富。喜欢倾听的人，一定不会拒绝任何一个认真思考问题的人，还能聆听很多人类心灵中最美、最伟大的观点，并且激发别人获得自信和勇气，这就是智慧。

千万不要抱着侥幸心理认为偶尔做一次见不得阳光的事无所谓，也不要认为自己智慧超群可以把那见不得人的事掩饰得天衣无缝、无人知晓。其实，自你心里刚升起做坏事的念头起，背运就已悄然走进你的生活，直到你接二连三倒霉时都不一定知道这都是因你心里滋生阴暗的结果。

温暖的语言可以拨动人的心弦，负能量的言语足以让人难堪。只要你摒弃了假话、大话、空话、脏话、下流话，你的天格、人格、地格的分量自然会随着语言场的改变而改变。

做人就做真实的自己，不要装腔作势摆谱，因为装出来的那个人根本不是真正的你。别人不说破，并不是你装出来的样子有多美，而是在看你演戏。

因一句不经意的话就会被伤到的人，一定是心胸狭隘并特别敏感的人。要想不经常“受伤”，努力做到凡事不计较。当你心胸宽阔，经常给周围的人带去阳光和安乐时，他们的言语自然就不再“带刺”，你也不会轻易“受伤”。

你喜欢的东西别人同样喜欢，你不喜欢的事情别人一样反感；如果你能把喜欢的东西送给别人，不喜欢的留给自己，届时你所得到的一定是别人望尘莫及的。

牢记别人对你的好，时刻不忘知恩图报；忘记自己对他人的好，时刻谨记助人而不求回报；由是，你会发现好事越来越多，忧伤越来越少。

所有诬陷、诽谤或者背后挑拨他人是非者，一定是心胸狭隘、妒忌心强的人。与这种人相处之道就是远离他们。

不要用语言掩饰自己的行为，也不要用行为掩饰自己的心念。因为只有内心有所顾忌时，你才会想方设法去掩饰自己的言行。

如果你想得到别人的尊重，请首先给予他人足够的尊重。如果你想拥有被爱的感觉，请先学会关爱对方。这不是简单的互换公式，但却是起码的行为规范。

有了选择，就必须学会取舍。当你有所选择时，得失就已开始在取舍中显现。

别舍不得给身边的人送去赞美的言辞和热烈的掌声。要知道，你所谓的付出不仅成就了他人，也提升了自己。

无论你做什么事，影子都会一辈子跟着你。走

正道是不怕影子歪的；爱你的人会无私地帮你，你也要学会奉献，传递爱，时时与人为善。

当违缘惹你发脾气时，请先冷静下来用心感受自己的呼吸。这时，你会发现自己呼吸的频率要超出运动时的很多倍。

生活中，当别人向你表达善意时，一定要欣然接受，并致以谢意。这样既成全了别人的真诚，同时自己也收获了接受善意的快乐。如果你简单粗暴、冷漠无情地拒绝或漠视了别人的好意，容易导致对方从此断了善念，关上行善之门。因为，一颗被误解的善心在创伤后是难以抚平的。

生命不但需要保持澎湃的激情，还需要阳光般

持续的原动力，才能在瞬息变幻中势不可挡，激流勇进！

请不要闯进别人的生活指手画脚，然后转身离开。用简单粗暴的方式给人上课，别人未必会理解。

在国家组织的重大活动面前，你能够积极参与并自觉遵守各项规定，做到不传谣、不添乱，时刻与国家利益、人民利益保持一致，说明你是一个真正明事理、识大体、爱祖国、有责任心的好公民。

如果你学会了克己容人，化解难题，那你已拥有了人生最宝贵的财富。

做事多替他人想，遇事必能得人助；做人做事存善念，睡觉做梦都吉祥。

碰见他人遭遇困难时，你要学会换位思考，不可取笑人家，更不能幸灾乐祸、落井下石。而是应当主动伸出友爱之手，去帮助他人度过难关。嘲笑别人者必被人嘲笑，援助他人者必得他人助力。

当你的观点和做法不被人理解时，请不要急于和对方辩解或争论。懂你的人无需去解释，默契就在那里；跟不懂你的人去探讨事物，纯属对牛弹琴。最好的方式是平心与其沟通，客观阐释自己的观点。

惯用严肃挑剔的态度对待亲近你的人，而装出热情友好的样子对待你厌恶的人，这两种表现不是所谓的成熟圆滑，而是黑白不分、自欺欺人。

感恩，就是感激别人给予的恩惠。感恩是一种生活态度，是一种责任与美德，更是一股催人向善的力量！以感恩的心面对周围的一切，就会活出人生的坦荡；能知恩图报，必能获得精彩；能以德报怨，终能成就人间大爱！

诞生，是人生的开始。死亡，是人生的终结。从始到终，如果你所做的事情都是善事，那你就圆通了为人之道。

冷漠的人不是生下来就冷漠，不是因为受过伤害，就是试图用冷漠来保护自己。

与他人刻意保持距离，也许你认为这是出于保护自己。可是这样，你难以得到对方的真心。

果农秋天摘柿子会剩几个挂在枝头，渔夫捕鱼会留下大鱼放生小鱼，猎人打猎从不伤害怀孕和刚出生的动物……若你明白以上做法都是有利于生物链不断、生态平衡的时候，请学会把自己的知识、财富、阳光、快乐无私分享给更多的人吧！

别人因事迟到而让你久久等待，你有事而延迟约定时间让别人白等一场的事儿，在我们生活中时有发生。千万不要因为别人的迟到而心生烦恼，也不要为自己不守时而寻找理由。要知道，守约守时是遵守承诺最起码的修行。

恶言伤人也伤己。为什么说有的人面如桃花，口如毒蝎？就是讲骂人者外表如花儿般美丽，但出口的恶言恶语如毒蝎一样在伤害周围的人。其实喜欢骂人者或在背后说别人坏话的人，自己一定没想到，听得最多的，伤得最深的其实是他本人。

当口出恶言成为习惯后，经由自己的耳朵日以继夜地聆听、灌输，久而久之，这种语言就成了心田的种子，早晚会结出恶运的果实。

语言是有声的思想，所以语言具有很强的振波。负能量的言辞就像小小的能量子弹，射入肉眼所不见的生命领域。虽看不见恶语的存在，但那些愤怒和怨恨的话已经发出振波，带着强势的负能量在伤人伤己，可怕的结果往往让人意想不到。如果你能把不开心时骂人、咄恶言的习性化为良言善语，那么这种无形正能量就会在不知不觉中改变你的情绪、心境和命运。

天性耿直不是缺点。与人沟通时只要不以一种态度走天下，必然不会处处碰壁。如能因地制宜，因人而异，即可四海通达。

水无言，却能利万物。阳光无言，但能给万物带来光明与生机。帮助他人虽无言，但他人却能感受到你的真诚与温暖。

自信和微笑不分国界，是打开国家外交和国际交流的金钥匙。

不要用你所谓的智慧去占善良人的便宜，不是

人家没看出你的小聪明，而是不屑与你计较。你也许认为自己得了便宜，其实人家收获的德行和福报恰恰是你所失去的。

学习认错，可使你免于做虚荣和面子的奴隶。认错不但不会失去什么，反而会让你增加容人之量。

真正能虚心接受意见的人，一定要有兼容并包的雅度。只要别人提的意见对，即使是别有用心，也要予以采纳。

靠欺骗获取的好处会远远少于失去的。所以古代成就王道者不欺骗天下，建立霸业者不欺骗邻国，善治国者不欺骗人民，善治家者不欺骗亲人。

恰切之助如人饮水，冷暖自知，有时，爱心助人也当讲求火候，热送清凉，冷送温暖。但求雪中送炭，不必锦上添花。

尺有所短，寸有所长。你可以扬长避短，更应该扬长补短。

不要认为凡事都是别人的错，自己才是对的。许多时候不认错也是一种错。

善良的人习惯站在对方的角度和立场看问题。在换位思考的过程中，你会看破许多别人所不能看破的东西，有意想不到的收获。

请不要执着于自己内心积存的负面信息，从而自寻烦恼，那些烦忧和不开心犹如用毛笔蘸水写在练字帖上的字，水干即逝。

不要轻信明星所谓生活隐私的偷拍和曝光，有时那是他们为了引发大众猎奇心理而自拍自炒的惯用方法。

黑暗里，无论多么微弱的灯光都会给人们带来无限的希望。白昼中，谁又会珍视给世界带来温暖和光明的阳光？更别谈那微弱的灯光了！

不要图一时口舌之快而吵架，因为吵架是双刃剑，会伤人伤己。

很多时候，人们喜欢用惯性思维去看得失，其实得失是守衡的。在短暂的人生路上，得失其实不重要，真正重要的是你撒播和传递阳光给人们带去光明和温暖的过程。

没有付诸于行动的感恩，还不是真正意义上的感恩！

人与人之间最贴切的安慰，就是站在他人的角度理解或分担其痛苦，并真诚陪伴他。

与其非议别人的不足，不如以其缺点为镜为鉴，来反省和完善自己的德行。

就一件事情而言，如果你不明晰情况，请不要

讲话。如果你喜欢发表言论，请在你知道情况后再讲。因为，不知而言为不智，知而不言为不忠。

知之为知之，不知为不知。不知而自以为知者，此乃愚者。

人们平时生气争吵时说出的很多话，大多数是积郁心中怨恨的惯性发泄或一时激愤不计后果的气话。当你冷静下来就会发现，原来那些气话伤人伤己，都是毒副作用很强的负面能量。所以，劝君注意和重视沟通频度和方式，不要试图用生气争吵的极端方式解决问题，因为人生气所造成的冲动伤害是一块难以去除且令人后悔莫及的伤疤。

人的微笑比衣着更重要。微笑就像穿过乌云的太阳，能照亮阴暗，给周围的人带去温暖。用微笑与人打招呼，对方可以感受到你的温暖和友善。

一个人最富足的快乐源于

阳光般无处不在的自由心性！还有随时随地发现、捕捉和欣赏美的能力。

别人对你态度的好坏，常常取决于你怎么对待别人。

只要你给别人带来的是无伪的阳光，根本不需你去强调和宣扬，大家心里都能感受到你的真诚、光明与温暖。

你在困境中首先寻求帮助的那个人，一定是你认为最能帮你，也是关系最好的朋友之一。对方如果毫不犹豫地帮助你，你一定要珍惜和感恩。如果因特殊情况没有帮你，请不要错怪朋友，也许他有难处。请你换位思考，生活中别人求助你时，你是真心给予帮助还是敷衍了事呢？

“敬酒”顾名思义就是以表达敬重和情谊为前提，如果强行劝酒超过限度就不再是一种有蕴涵的文化表现，而演变成了伤身、伤情的陋习。

做事不光明磊落，生怕让人知道的事儿就是苟且之事；自己不愿做善事，还找理由阻挠他人做善事的人非善人；做事不靠谱儿，还总是背后传播他人缺点、事事算计别人的人是小人。

当别人的决定已成事实时，不要追问人家为什么？既然问与不问都已成事实，最好的办法就是默默关心、深深祝福，能够支持多少就去积极行动。

谣言止于智者。当听到谣言时，先不要急于去批判或否定中枪的人，而是要静心思考传谣者的目的。你要做的不是去判断谣言的真假，而是从你那儿开始制止谣言不再传播。因为每一次谣言的传播，受伤的不仅是中枪者本人，也会迷惑人心，扰乱事实。如果你能不求回报地第一时间把谣言内容告诉中枪者，并帮助化解，那你的心灵会增添了一份厚度。

在飞机场候机时间过长时，请不要怨声载道，也不要对工作人员大声喊叫或者做出一些不理智的行为，因为这些无用的努力不但无法让你按时登机，还会影响你的心情，干扰他人的状态。

有故事的人，沉静而简单；肤浅单薄的人，浮躁而不安。遇到任何事情要学会冷静思考、简单处世 ，此心不动，随机而动。

发自内心的微笑没有国界、不分地域、不限性别……微笑，不仅可以改变僵局，还可以化解矛

盾、误解。请带着你的微笑，去关照、感化、影响周围的磁场，让你身边所有人的脸上都洋溢着不落的笑容。

你想对别人行善施爱的时候，请不要太刻意，如果过分刻意表现会导致对方感受不到你的好意而是压力。

能让你瞬间暴躁如雷的事情，一定是你最敏感的事情，也是你内心最不愿意提及的事情。如果你能静心观察反思自己为何那么在意这件事，你就不会那么执着、敏感或脆弱。因为，就在你生气时，自己的弱点已经暴露无遗。

人越简单，福气就越多；你有多少是非，就有多少痛苦。跟我们简单相交而没有目的的人，一定不讲是非；而与你搬弄别人是非的人，必是是非之人。远离是非之人，你的心灵才会还原到那一尘不

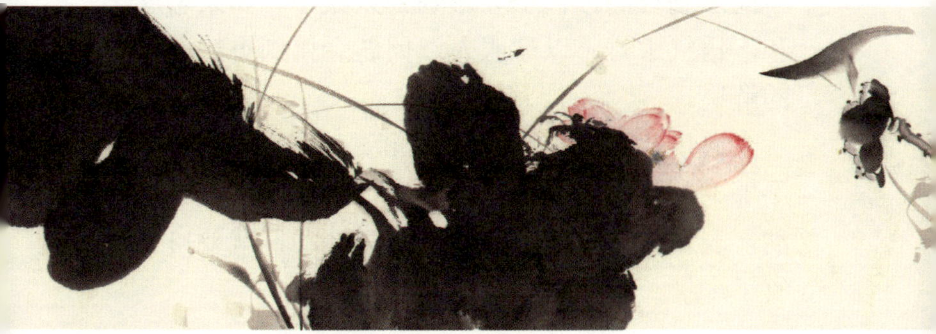

染的纯净空间。

是非之人传递是非之事。如果听进了是非之言，你就中了是非之人的病毒。这时，你必然会为是非之事买单。而且，无论你买不买单都已被是非之人所利用。

人在吵架时，恶毒犀利言辞带给对方的伤害，远远超出肉体的创伤。

候车室里的座位无论你占多少个，都是一时的，车来了你都必须离开。人生纵有很多位置留给你，无论哪个阶段也只有一个最适合你，其余都将留给他人。

当你陷入左右为难、难于抉择的困局时，请不要去抱怨与责怪他人和外界，此时更重要的是平和心态、搁置争议，理性地思考如何更有利于大局而不应该仅仅考虑一己得失！

带着感恩的心去爱恋人，将收获纯美的爱情；秉持感恩的心去爱生活，将收获丰沛的人生。

在公共场合高声喧哗与争吵，既有失风度又不能达到目的，甚至会影响公共秩序。如果态度平和，语气中肯，以理服人，问题会得到更快、更好的解决。

遇事急于下结论，盲目冲动，说明你的心胸还不够大、包容心不够宽广、心性不够成熟。适时冲动，表示你对生活有激情；时时冲动，就要自我检省了。

开口前先开动大脑，不可信口图一时痛快。管好口舌，谨言敏行，不扬人恶，自然你的朋友会多于敌人。

因一次没有被他“合理利用”，就对你恶语相向、制造事非之人，免受其更大伤害的方法就是敬而远之，因为在他伪善的华丽外衣之下是逐利，你的选择就是擦亮眼睛，不与狼共舞！

你无法忘记别人的过，就永远看不到自己的错。与其抱怨别人的短处，不如反省自己的不足。

做人的本真是善良和心的自由，如果不择手段为了获取名利而丧失掉本性，即使得到也是负累。

当你把灿烂的笑容绽放于世间时，你收获的是幸福愉悦；如若你把冷漠的目光投给别人，你的世界已然布满冰霜。

当你的见解与大家的观点相左时，请不必心生疑惑或妄自菲薄。客观坦然表达观点，真诚热情沟通就是可敬可赞的行为。

想要给对方留下完美印象，第一步是欢喜地记住对方的名字。

有些烦恼是庸人自扰，源于你不清楚自己是谁、要什么，为什么做。一味盲目追求那些并不适合你且一生无法达到的东西，是不满的源头。

当虚荣心牵引你借着他人的名望、世俗的头衔把个人身份或形象抬得很高时，请提前给自己准备好一块能让你摔倒时防止受伤的海绵垫儿。

即便你的热情换来他人的冷漠，也不要由此降低你的热情。这不是因为对方习惯冷漠，只是他害怕被有目的的热情所伤害。如果有一天你的热情不再被外界的冷漠、丑陋的言行所干扰时，那么你的热情已升华为闪耀着理性光辉的大爱！

请勿出于个人偏见，冒然评判他人的好坏。你知道他的故事，未必深谙故事背后的成因；你可能听闻过关于他的评价，但没有亲历他曾经的挣扎与磨难；或许你了解他的不幸，却无法体验他的痛苦。那么，尽可能善待并理解他人，这也是在松绑和开释自己。

价值观不一致时不要勉强别人做你觉得“应该”的事情，当你想去改变别人的念头出现时，对方自我反抗的磁场也已瞬间形成。

有的时候，沉默不是逃避，而是为了缓解或化解他人的执着与偏见。

只要你心里充满爱，所有人都是你的贵人，你也是所有人的贵人。

喜欢把自己的烦恼全倒给别人的人，就是所谓的“垃圾人”。人生活在世间，不可能没有烦恼。善于自我调整，消除烦恼污垢是智者。反之习惯把精神垃圾送给别人的人，不但解决不了问题，还会给他人带去障碍。我们既要做智者，还要远离垃圾人。

喜欢你的人，会把你身上所有的表现都看成优点，不喜欢你的人，往往把你的缺点放大。

把温暖送给懂得感恩的人，这份爱会传递得更远；有时给冷漠而自私的人送温暖，他不但不会感恩，还误以为你有所图。所以，帮人也要有所选择。

在成长的过程中，要学会感谢所有在你生命里出现过的人，是他们成就了现在或未来的你。

当别人真诚待你，请不要故意摆谱。摆谱不会提高你的层次，反而降低你的水平。

永远不要跟你不熟悉的人说太多关于你的故事，多说无益。也许，因为一句无意或善意的语言，对方却由此记恨在心。那本不该出现的违缘、烦恼、阻碍就会随之而来。

学习他人之长本是件好事，但千万不要因为学习别人而丢失自己。

坦荡做人不算计别人，因为你每算计别人一次就会消减一次自己的福报。

不要过于掩饰自己的错误，当你竭力掩饰自身问题时，就不经意地出卖和远离了本我。

无论你能攀登多高，都高不过天。身居高处，不要看不起比自己位低的人，尽可能给他们创造攀登进取的机会。只有做到了这一点，你的灵魂看起来才能和你的位置一样尊贵。

强加给别人的好心有时对别人来说是压力。把这份好心换成理解和尊重，对方就会欣然接受。

不要轻易羡慕别人的风光和幸福，也许对方在某些方面还不如你如意。人都习惯把美好的一面展示给别人，而自己却在默默地承受无形或有形的压力。

有人说：“你叫不醒的永远不是熟睡中的人，而是装睡的人。”面对装睡的人，看是否有叫醒他

的必要，如果没有必要就把他锁屋里，直到对方装不下去为止；或者，躺对方身边和他一起装睡，直到他醒来。

朋友互赠礼物是礼节，若送就送自己能力范围内最好的。千万不可送过期的食物或日用品，也许因为你的粗心大意，伤了朋友之间的友谊。

心眼小的人喜欢怨天尤人，会神经质地认为别人都在针对他（她）。心胸开阔的人从不抱怨，更不会斤斤计较、患得患失。心灵博大，空灵无物才能恬淡安静。

不要总盯着别人劳动换来的果实不放手，要学会体察他人成果背后的艰辛。故有君子不贪他人之食，小人好夺别人成果之说。

真相不真，因果不空。人们所有追求的真相都是

内心的执着与理想，其实任何真相背后还会有更多个真相存在。而这些真相只不过是说服你的一个理由而已，你又何须苦苦去寻求那虚而不真的真相呢？

无论多么有爱心，为爱付出多少努力，若你爱的方式不能被需要的人接纳，就需要反思。爱是彼此开心，共享福光。而不是一厢情愿，强加于人。

人生无常，唯有随时适应变化，才不会被变化所弃置。

远离怨恨最好的方法是严以律己，宽以待人。

得到的多，付出的少就会得“病”。付出而不求回报得多，“病”就会少。

真正做善事的人，从不夸赞自己所做的好事，而是默默地撒播爱心。

一个人的能力，靠嘴巴是吹不出来的，主要靠行动实践来证明。

同一个行业出现竞争才能激发精品意识，提高产品的质量。所以智慧的人永远都在赞美竞争对手，并向对手学习。而愚蠢的人除了排挤、诽谤竞争对手之外，还会给竞争对手制造麻烦。

世间万物有实相也皆有虚相，不论你的念所对虚相还是实相，对方皆有感应。

人如果没有德行，那他所有的能力最终将会归零。若注重德行的培养，所做之事都会顺利吉祥。

放下对别人的偏见，持正知正见待人处事。当不再执着别人的错误，就会减掉内心负面的包袱。

简单为易，复杂是琐。两边莫走，直行中间。

不必用挑剔的眼光去看别人，这是嫉妒心在作怪。挑剔不能抬高自己的身价，反而成就对方的胸怀。

能为人所用说明有价值，会用人证明有才智。世界上其实不缺干活的，而少用智慧带大家干好活，做好事，做好人的人。

做人就做内心自在的人，既不委屈求全，也不专横跋扈；既不攀龙附凤，也不强颜欢笑。这样才能人生洒脱，人间自在。

如果你被别人抛弃，说明对方没有眼光。如果你再把自己抛弃，证明对方确实很有眼光。

不夸赞自己的所长，也不指责别人的不足。要明白，你有长一寸的优点，就有短一寸的缺点。别人又何尝不是呢？

每天欢喜，周围的人也因你而欢喜。每天忧伤，身边的人会感受到你的低落。情绪决定环境，环境决定健康，健康决定生命。

唯真正懂得谦让，才具有做事不纠结的智慧。

越渴望交际说明你内心越孤独，内心越孤独才越喜欢应酬。其实，交际和应酬不是孤独的解药。只有忘掉自己，才能了解自己。只有懂得利他，才会斩断孤独源头。

处世多思是好事，但过分了也不尽善。

好心用到正确的地方才能变好事，好事给予需要的人才算是好人。

你只是一个个体，永远不要凌驾于大自然之上。 以大自然包容人类的胸怀去包容别人吧！

每个人都有他（她）自己的秘密，这个秘密就是他（她）自己的底线，也是最容不得人肆意冒犯的。所以，你要不想失去对方，就不要去打探他（她）的隐私，触犯他（她）的底线。

能看到他人的优点，他人就会看到你的智慧。能发现别人的缺点，别人就会看到你的愚昧。

把复杂的问题简单化是智慧，把简单的问题复杂化是愚蠢。

人要有包容之量，但不能有纵容之心。

如果你的善良被人误伤了，请不要介怀，也不要抱怨。也许，那只是因为当时缺少用智慧去行善的方法。

懂得感恩，爱才可以良性循环。

一诺千金决不能轻易改变。如果为了私欲改变承诺，私欲将改变你的一生。

有一种爱不需表达，其实对方都彼此知道。只要内心纯洁，不存私利，这份爱和友谊就能久而不变。

和父母提各种要求时，请先扪心自问自己曾为父母做过什么？

做人最大的悲哀是明明知道自己错了，还故意用虚伪的行为去掩饰过错。

坚持做正确的事情，总有一天会看到不一样的自己。

一句赞美不费吹灰之力，但对于被赞美的人而言可能产生不可思议的鼓励。当学会赞美别人时，身上就多了一个优点。

他人因受惠于你的帮助而真诚致谢时无须拒绝，倘若无意答谢也不可开口索要。

珍惜值得的人，会增加幸福的感觉，不去执着于不值得的人，会减少很多烦恼。

自以为是，容易固步自封。放下架子，迈开步子，往远处看，会发现广阔天地更多的美。

习惯做事给别人留后路的人，当自己遇到困难时常会迎刃而解。

能用行动去表达爱的方式就无须用太多华丽的语言，因为真正的爱在细微之处见真章。

不要习惯性地把承诺当作口头禅，只许诺而不兑现是言而无信的表现。

强势是一种病，如果不及早觉悟和自治，终究会在病痛中迷失自我。

有事情想不通时，请站在对方的角度去观省。在执着时，所有事物发展的频率几乎都会停留在利己的层次。

在还未真正了解别人意图时，请勿随意评论。除非能洞察全局，心通他意。

虽说赠人玫瑰手留余香，但要先有玫瑰，才能予人。

智者不拿望远镜看他人的过失，而是用放大镜观己不足。

欺骗别人是狡猾，欺骗自己是愚蠢、愚痴，所以要诚实地面对自心，不欺人，不自欺。

智者，从不夸夸其谈，最有智慧的言说是拈花一笑。 成大器者，都会隐忍质朴、不张狂不卖弄。

不要用你所谓的道理去教育别人，也不要用别人所谓的道理来束缚自己。因为你不在道中，不能

明其理。多换位思考，多勤思洞见，才能明白真正的道理。

心量不宽，难容于众。小事不忍，必生大患。

人人向往自由自在的生活，尤其是不喜欢墨守成规之人更渴望追求自由。不过，天下没有绝对的自由。唯有放下内心虚妄的执着、欲望，才能真正获得精神上的自由。

能给予真心的是不求回报之人，虚情假意者大都另有所图。

越害怕失去，越难以得到。越喜欢布施，反而常拥有。

做人过于功利，将会被功利所左右;做事过于激进，将会因激进而滋生障碍。你的目的他人心知肚明，只是不说破而已。

任何事情都有生有灭，只是时间长短不一而已。所以，万事随缘即可，切勿逆天而行。

不随意揣度别人，是做人最基本的修养。因为，你不是他，不可能真正理解他的生活，及其喜怒哀乐。也许你所认为的幸福对他来说一文不值，也许你所认为的痛苦对他而言是甘之如饴。

能看清自己，常常能看清他人，照破烦恼。能看清他人，未必能看清自己，了知当下。

习惯给别人台阶下的人，人生之路常畅通无阻。

想得到别人的信任，首先要做一个守信的人。切记，一次不守信将葬送你所有的信用额度。

勿从自身标准去评判他人，也别用他人的要求去苛求自己。 每个人的自身条件有别，做人做事的方法和标准也各不相同。

莫因无利可图，不屑于做举手之劳的利他人之事。莫为贪图一时之利，而损公肥私。

真爱无私，假爱多欲。不要假借爱之名去行自私之事，也不要拿自私之心去混淆世间真爱。

喜欢为错误找理由的人，迟早因自己的错误而丧失本我。

当思维只停留在事物表面时，请先不要急于发言。沉默不语才会让你更加清楚事物的本质。

美好的祝福不一定能成真，但消极的担忧念叨多了，反而变成事实。生活中要多祝福，少担忧。

带着烦恼生活，烦恼无数，带着快乐生活，快乐无边。

自视优秀的人容易被自己的眼界和见识所局限。真正优秀的人总能发现或找到比自己更优秀的人，不断进取和成长。

只要心怀感恩，会常遇善缘。反之，恶缘不断，直到明理为止。

宽容是修养，纵容是无知。

能讲真心话的，不一定是家人，但一定是值得珍惜的人。

若不善于同妄念、欲望作斗争，很难走上光明而正确的人生轨道。

若真心无法打动你认为重要的人时，请将真心换无心，或许有意外之收获。

真正有能力的人不会傲慢无礼，而是谦虚有度。

控制得了情绪的人能占主动，而无法控制情绪

的人注定陷入被动。

万事没有如果，既然做了就无需后悔。因为，无论何种结果都是最好的安排。

莫要抱怨环境不利于成长，栋梁之才在任何环境下都能把潜能发挥到极致。

清清白白的你如平白遭人诽谤，请一定保持沉着冷静。因为清者自清，无需与任何人做过多解释。

喜欢自卖自夸的善非真善，因为真善无需向任何人夸赞。

凡事善于换位思考的人懂得体谅他人的不易；喜欢站在自己的角度看问题的人，只看到他人的不足，忽视了自己的缺点。

常常抱怨运气不顺的人一定要反思自己的行为，当决定改变自己的行为，让善念升起之时，正是好运开始之日。

爱一个人不是天天把爱挂在嘴边，而是把爱化作动力融汇在生活中的点点滴滴，让所爱的人感受到你发自内心的真诚与关爱。

出身不是自己能决定的，但做一个什么样的人却是自己可以决定的。

无论何时，心存善念，各种善缘皆会出现在周围。

不强加给别人不需要的，给予别人最想要的是修养，也是智慧。

把善良和慈悲分享给所有善良的人并不是你有分别心，而是这样的选择让你远离了不善之人。

人有瑕疵和疾患并不可怕，可怕的是道德底线和责任感的缺失。

高品质的生活状态并非独属于经济实力雄厚的人，知足简约的人更容易享有。

简约是一种习惯，也是一种精神。当生活过得越来越简约时，你会发现生活的真谛。

白天所有真实发生过的事情貌似真的，过去之后又如过眼烟云。晚上在梦里上演的事看似假的，但到眼前又是如此真实。其实无论真也好，假也罢，都是人生梦境，根本无须执着。

说话不要刻薄，因为刻薄克的是自己。倒水不要倒满，因为水满则溢。

一味地在物质上富养孩子，一味地满足孩子的物质要求，只会养出一个没有金钱观念，不懂自我奋斗，只会依靠父母的孩子。

一个人的力量是微小的，很多人在一起每人丢一根柴火也能燃起熊熊火焰，这个“众”字阐释了整个人生的大小道理。

You can ask for help from friends for something you can't manage, but should refrain from doing so for things you don't like to do. This is friendship's biggest taboo.

Being a warm-hearted human being is a good thing, but it does not mean that you should agree to help with whatever you are asked. A warm-hearted person should not only be good at helping others, but also learn how to refuse to do what they are unable to do.

Don't make the mistake of believing that after earning the praise of a few, you'll be recognized by all. As a matter of fact, people who recognize you may not praise you face to face, and vice versa.

Those who like to criticize others must consider themselves to be perfect, but they don't know that, in fact, criticizing others is a fatal flaw in human nature.

Some people get hurt by the truth because they are used to listening to lies.

When you are angry, remain silent and make no decision, because all decisions made when angry are unreasonable.

It is hypocritical and dishonest to take no actions due to incompetence after promising to help others. Because of such a behavior, others may miss their chance to succeed.

Unselfishness is not just a fine word. Instead, it means you volunteer to do things and seek nothing in return. If you get upset or start complaining that your help yields no reward, it simply indicates that you have a selfish heart. Otherwise, you won't be troubled at all.

Those who ask for your calligraphy or paintings must really appreciate you and think that they have a close relationship with you. If you have to fix a price for your work and have those people pay for them, it becomes tacky. Those with gratitude will not take your work for free.

When someone tries to gossip with you about the private matters of others, you must stop it there. Otherwise, you will be the next subject of gossip.

Different opinions are inevitable in interpersonal communications. So is an argument. However, no matter how angry you are, don't swear or make personal attacks because it will hurt others as well as you.

Learn to communicate with others in a gentle way. Don't throw your temper at others. You've got to understand that no one owes you anything in this world.

If you always fight for the first, you will fall onto a wrong path, which won't help you move forward. If you insist on conducting yourself in a sophisticated way and letting others move ahead, then you will be able to move along with good people and find the bright world together with them.

In spare time, don't be keen on prying into others' gossip as it will not only bring you no good but also harm you. When you no longer talk about others' mistakes or privacy, troubles and anger will disappear naturally.

You can't prove yourself to be knowledgeable no matter how many books you have collected. Those who are truly knowledgeable never show off their book collection or brag about their reading.

The virtue of those who are used to offering others help, giving praise and passing a smile will accumulate. On the contrary,

the virtue of those who can help others but do nothing and vise versa will be impaired.

When you see something you consider unreasonable, keep your mouth shut first. Be silent and observe for a while, you will then find out that things are not as simple as what you have thought.

When one knows something is wrong but still looks for reasons to absolve himself from blame, he has already disgraced himself, even though all he was trying to do was save face and dignity.

When others do something wrong, you can analyze for them and give them some advice for improvement, but you can't expose their defects. Exposing others' weaknesses, impeding their future and compromising their reputation are not conduct of a gentleman.

Those who put on airs in order to get respect from others will not necessarily get others' genuine respect. And those who pretend

to respect others must want something from others.

When someone is unwilling to talk about their past or are keeping it private, don't keep asking. Such behavior is a nuisance for others.

Do not sacrifice morality for your own benefit, even worse so would be to sacrifice credibility. The benefits that everyone can see are already no longer of use.

Being too clever makes people stupid because such people will always think about their personal gains first; on the contrary, those with wisdom think about others' gains and losses first.

Even if you see something through, don't point it out. The

more courtesies you give others, the more room there will be for you to progress.

Are there any so-called secrets in the world? In fact, there are no more secrets as soon as you know the truth of something.

Don't speculate about others' thoughts based on your own ideas, as it is the root of misunderstanding.

When dealing with others, first think about what others can gain from you instead of what you can get from them. Losses and gains are directly proportional, so don't even think about gaining without losing.

Always think about how nice others are to you instead of how nice you are to them, and your gratitude will be enhanced, and you won't complain about others' minor mistakes either.

Sometimes, if you stick to things you should do but you don't want to do, you may unexpectedly get what you want.

When you are suspicious of someone doing something, don't continue your course with him because things have quietly changed since you have doubt.

Don't give remarks that would enable others to make groundless accusations out of thin air. Perhaps, your casual jokes will do great harm to others.

Those who like to pry on or talk about others' privacy must not know that their own privacy, in fact, has been known to all.

Remarks you get from others when they are angry or unreasonable are worth considering. Those remarks might be unpleasant but most pertinent thoughts about you.

Those who scheme against others all the time will, sooner or later, exhaust their wits and pay the price themselves at the end.

If you do good things, all good people around you will be closer to you. But if you harbor bad thoughts, both your luck and good friends will leave you.

Language garbage generated from negative words have accumulated around you since you know how to speak. You must correct this bad habit and clear your language garbage in time. Only then can you obtain colorful energy space and language power.

When two eggs collide, the one exerts power first must break first. This rule tells us that those who like to start a fight or war must end up losing.

Everyone has merits and demerits. Therefore, when you deal with others, don't magnify their merits out of happiness or magnify their demerits out of annoyance.

To get something, you have to give something up first. If you can give something great up, you can get something great; if you can give something trivial up, you can get something trivial; if you can give nothing up, you can get nothing.

If people and nations can communicate with each other in a peaceful way, then we will realize peaceful coexistence at the end.

When someone good at picking up a fight instills you with negative thoughts, don't act impulsively or even do anything that will make you regret. This is because only those who can control their emotions can prevent themselves from easily being used by others and thus stay away from faults.

To forgive is being kind to yourself; to hold a grudge is to punish yourself.

Promises are both light and heavy. They are heavy when you keep your promises in mind and do your best to realize them; they are light when you forget others' promises to you and let things be the way they should be.

I will not say a word about what I don't know; if you do know something, then say something about it. Knowing nothing is not horrible, while pretending to know is.

If you are used to listening to others, you will possess the most precious treasure in the world. Those who like to listen to others will never turn down serious thinkers, and thus they can hear some of the most beautiful and greatest thoughts within the human heart. They can even make others confident and courageous, and this is wisdom.

Don't take your chance to try anything bad, thinking that one bad thing will not matter; also, don't think that your witted brain can hide the bad things you have done so that no one will ever find out. In fact, bad luck has come into your life the moment your thought arises to do something bad. You may not know that all the bad things happening to you thereafter are results of the darkness in your heart.

Warm words can touch people's hearts while negative words would embarrass people. When you get rid of lies, big talks, hollow words, swearing and nasty words, your destiny, personality and fate will change accordingly.

We have to be who we really are. Don't put on an act because that's not the real you anyway. Others may not point it out. It is not because you have an excellent act, but because they regard your behavior as a show.

One who gets hurt by mindless words must be narrow-minded and sensitive. If you don't want to get hurt so often, you must try to let things go. When you become broad-minded, you will bring sunshine, peace and happiness to others. With no more thorns in their words, you will not get hurt easily.

Others might like things you like; they may also dislike what you dislike. If you can give what you like to others and keep what you dislike to yourself, then what you get must be something others desire but are out of their reach.

Keep the kindness of others in your mind and try to repay it all the time. Forget your kindness to others and never want them to pay you back. Doing so, you will discover that good things will happen more and worries become less.

All those who frame others up, slander others or spread

rumors must be narrow-minded and jealous. The best way to deal with them is to stay away from them.

Don't conceal your behavior with words; don't conceal your words with behavior either, because you will only do so when you have apprehension in your heart.

If you want to be respected, you have to respect others first. If you want to be loved, love others first. These are not simple exchanges, but the basic rules for conduct.

Where there are options, there is weighing. When you make a choice, losses and gains will arise.

Don't refrain yourself from praising or applauding others. You should know that your so-called efforts not only make them who they are but also improve yourself.

No matter what you do, your shadow will always follow you. The shadow will never be crooked so long as you take the right path. People who love you will help you selflessly. You should also learn to give, to pass on love and be kind to everyone always.

When something or someone irritates you, calm down and listen to your breathing attentively. You will find that the frequency of your breathing is many times faster than that when you do exercise.

In daily life, when someone expresses kindness to you, do accept it and thank him. In this way, you not only fulfill his sincerity, but also receive the happiness of accepting his kindness. But if you reject his kind heart brutally and indifferently, he might shut down the door to kindness from then on, as it is hard for someone to ease the pain after being misunderstood by others.

One needs to stay both passionate and energetic. Only in this way can he become irresistible and move forward.

Don't break into others' lives to make remarks only to turn around and leave. People may not understand this simple and rude way of lecturing.

You are a good, patriotic, reasonable, and responsible citizen if you actively participate in major national events, abide by all the stipulations and keep your interests consistent with those of the nation and people without spreading rumors or making trouble.

If you learn to restrain yourself and tolerate others, and solve difficult problems, you have possessed the most valuable treasure in your life.

Think of others no matter what you do, and you will get help when you need it; keep a good heart and kind thoughts no matter what you do, and you will have good dreams when you sleep.

When encountering others going through difficulties, you should learn to put yourself in their shoes, lend a hand, and help them go through the hard time. You can't make fun of them or gloat. Those who laugh at others will be laughed at one day; those who help others will be helped by others.

When your views and practices are not understood, don't jump in and defend yourself or argue. To those who understand you, there is no need to explain. To those who do not, it is just like casting pearls before swine. The best way is to communicate with calmness and express your views objectively.

Being serious and critical to those close to you and putting

on a warm and friendly look at those you hate does not make you mature or sophisticated; on the contrary it shows how you can't tell right from wrong and how you are fooling yourself.

Gratitude means to be grateful for things others give you. It is an attitude for life, a kind of responsibility and virtue, and a force to improve yourself. When you face everything with gratitude, your life will be magnanimous; when you are always grateful to others and repay them, your life will be wonderful; if you forgive others with kindness, you will make contributions to human benevolence.

Life starts from birth and ends at death. From the beginning to the end, if all you have done is good, then you have acquired the rules of human conduct.

Aloof people are not born aloof. They are the way they are either because they have gotten hurt, or because they are shielding

themselves with aloofness.

You may think that you are protecting yourself when you deliberately distance yourself from others, but when you do this, no one will be true to you.

Farmers will leave some on branches when they pick persimmons in autumn; fishermen will set little fish free and only keep the big ones; and hunters never hunt pregnant animals or cubs. If you realize that these are conducive to the food chain and the ecological balance, please share your knowledge, wealth and happiness selflessly with more people.

When others arrive late, you may have to wait for some time; when you get occupied by something unexpected, you may have to blow someone off. Things like these happen from time to time. So, don't get upset because someone is late, or find excuses for your unpunctuality. Know this, being on time is the basic cultivation to honor your promises.

Malicious words hurt others as well as oneself. Those who curse others may be as beautiful as flowers on the outside, but their malicious words are as poisonous as scorpions. In fact, those who like to curse people behind their people's back don't know that the malicious words are mostly heard by themselves and those words hurt themselves even deeper.

When swearing becomes a habit, you will hear it day and night. Gradually, it becomes a seed buried in your heart, and it will bear the fruit of bad luck to you one day.

Words are sounds with thoughts; therefore, they have a strong vibration. Words with negative energy are like bullets that can shoot into areas of life that a naked eye does not see. Though we can't see the existence of malicious words, the words have given out vibrations with negative energy and hurt everyone including the ones who curse. This often leads to unexpected terrible results. If you can convert your malicious words into good ones, your mood, mentality and destiny will be changed by this imperceptible force.

Upright nature is not a weakness. As long as you don't deal with people with one same attitude or manner, things won't be difficult all the time. If you deal with others in accordance with their differences, you will be able to deal with everyone.

Water benefits all creatures without saying any words; the sun brings light and vitality to all creatures without saying any words; even though you help others without saying any words, they will be able to feel your warmth and sincerity.

Without national boundaries, smile and confidence are the golden key to international communication and diplomacy.

Don't use your wits to take advantage of good people; they don't fuss about it not because they don't see what you did. You may think that you have gained extra advantage, but, in fact, the virtue merits and blessings others have gained are precisely what you have lost.

Learning to apologize can keep you from being a slave of vanity and dignity. It won't cost you anything. Instead, it will make you a more tolerant and forgiving person.

Those who can really accept others' advice must have the demeanor to embrace diversity. You should accept others' advice if they are right, even though the others might have their own motives.

What you lose will outweigh what you gain from deception. Therefore, in ancient times, good emperors did not deceive the world; good conquerors did not deceive neighboring countries; good leaders did not deceive people, and good men did not deceive families.

Help in need is like water. Only the one who drinks it knows whether it is cold or warm. At times, you should think about the necessity when offering help. Don't make your help supplementary; make it indispensable.

Everyone has his own disadvantages. You can avoid your weaknesses, but you should work on them.

Don't blame everything on other people, thinking that you are always right. Most of the time, not admitting your mistakes is a huge mistake.

Kind-hearted people often see things from others' perspectives. Doing so, you will be able to see through many vanities that others can't see through and receive unexpected gains.

Don't be obsessed with negative information accumulated in mind and thus ask for trouble. Trouble and unhappiness are like the characters written on a copybook for calligraphy practice using water, gone with the time as water dries up.

Don't believe celebrities' so-called privacy exposed by hidden cameras. Sometimes it is a common way they use to arouse and attract more attention.

When we are in darkness, light would always give us hope, however dim it is; while in daytime, who will be grateful to the sun that brings warmth and light to the world? Much less to the dim lamplight.

Don't argue to get short-term pleasure because argument is a double-edged sword; it hurts others as well as yourself.

Most of the time, people like to think about losses and gains through a habitual thinking model. In fact, losses and gains are always balanced. In the short course of life, what is important is the process of bringing light and warmth to people around, rather than gains or losses.

Gratitude without action is not true gratitude.

The best comfort for others is to see things from their perspectives, understand and lessen their pains, and truly accompany them.

Rather than talking about others' weaknesses, we should

reflect on and improve ourselves based on their weaknesses.

Don't talk about a matter at hand if you are unclear of what is going on . If you like to give comments, do it after you learn about the situation. It is unwise to say something you don't know, just as it is disloyal not to say something you do know.

Be honest with what you know and what you don't. It is foolish to think that you know something you actually don't.

Most words we say when we quarrel with others are resentment and mean words that we let out without thinking about the consequences. But when you calm down, you will realize that all those words hurt others as well as yourself, and that they emit negative energy with strong side effects. Therefore, please pay attention to your way and frequency of communicating with others; don't solve problems by quarreling because the harm we create when we are angry will be the worst and most regretful scar in our life.

A smile is more important than what you wear. A smile is just like the sun that shines through dark clouds and brings light to darkness. Greeting others with a smile, and from your smile, they will feel the warmth and friendliness.

A person's ultimate happiness comes from his free heart that is like the ubiquitous Sun and his ability to find and enjoy the beauty of life.

The way others treat you often depends on how you treat them.

You don't have to emphasize or advertise it if what you bring others is true sunshine, as everyone can feel the warmth in their heart.

The ones you turn to first when you are in trouble must be those who you think can help you the most and are close to you. If they help you without hesitation, then you really need to cherish and be grateful to them. If they can't help you for some reason, don't blame them. Perhaps they have their own difficulties. And do think about this - when others ask for your help, do you help them with sincerity or simply go through motions?

The premise of a toast is respect and friendship. When someone is forced to drink excessively, then the toast has already become a bad habit instead of a cultural expression.

Things you fear to be known by others are bad things; people who not only don't do good deeds but also stop others from doing so are bad people; people who are not only irresponsible but also spread rumors about others' weaknesses and schemes against others are mean people.

When others' decisions have become fact, don't ask them why because things have become the way they are regardless of being asked or not. The best way is to care and bless others quietly and provide as much support as one can.

Wise men end rumors. When you hear rumors, don't judge or deny the parties concerned. Instead, you should consider the purpose of the rumor spreaders. You don't need to tell the rumors from true and false, and you just need to stop them from further spreading because every single spread of the rumors hurts not only the parties concerned but also confuse people and the truth. If you tell the parties concerned at once without seeking for return and help

resolve the issue, your heart will get fuller.

Even if you wait in the airport for a long time, don't complain, yell at the crew members or do anything unreasonable. This is because not only can't these useless efforts enable you to check-in on time, but they will also affect your mood and disturb other people.

Grounded men are always serene and simple, while superficial men are always restless. Therefore, whatever happens, don't get restless. Learn to think calmly and treat things with serenity. Keep a serene heart and only move when the opportunity is suitable.

A real smile within one's heart has nothing to do with boundaries, regions or sexes. It can not only change a stalemate, but also resolve conflicts and misunderstandings. Therefore, please care for, move and affect others with your smile; please let people around you wear a big smile.

When you want to be good to other people, don't do it deliberately because if you do so, what other people sense is not your kindness but pressure from you.

Things that can irritate you in a flash must be the most sensitive issues for you, which you don't want to mention at all. If you can calm down and think about why you care about those things so much, you will no longer be that obsessed, sensitive or weak because when you get angry, you have totally exposed your weaknesses.

The simpler one is, the more blessing he has; the more gossip one generates, the more suffering one has. Those who make friends with you without a purpose can't be the ones who would gossip; those who gossip in front of you must be trouble makers themselves.

If your heart wants to return to the dustless pure space, you have to get away from gossip first.

A gossiper spreads gossip. If you take it in, you will be infected by such a virus, and inevitably pay for it because, one way or another, you have been used by a gossiper.

Malicious words to others during a fight hurt more than physical injuries.

No matter how many seats you occupy in the waiting room, you can't hold on to them forever, as you have to leave when the train arrives. Though there are many seats, there is only a suitable one in every phase of your life. And you will pass the rest on to others eventually.

When you are in a dilemma and don't know what decisions to make, don't blame others or the world, because what's more important at this point is to keep calm and postpone disputes. You should see the big picture in a reasonable way instead of thinking about your own losses and gains.

If you love your partner with gratitude, you will obtain abundant love. If you love your life with gratitude, you will obtain a full life.

Arguing loudly with others in public can't get you anything but make you ungracious. What's worse, it will even affect the public order. Problems will be solved faster and better if you deal with others with a nice attitude, a gentle tone and reasons.

Jumping to a conclusion easily means that you are not mature or tolerant enough. Acting on impulse occasionally means that you still have passion for life. Always being impulsive shows that it is time you do some self-reflection.

Think before you say anything, and never say things for a moment of pleasure. You will get more friends than enemies when you watch your mouth, keep attentive, and spread no gossip.

If someone says malicious things to you or makes up gossip about you for he didn't get to use you, stay away from him before he causes you greater harm. Under his luxuriant disguise is vanity. So what you need to do is to sharpen your eyes, and never dance with wolves.

If you can't forgive others, you can never see your mistakes. Reflect on your own weaknesses rather than complain about those of others.

Kindness and a free heart are human nature. If one loses his kind nature when he does whatever it takes to get fame and wealth, his losses will outweigh his gains.

When you give the world a beautiful smile, you will receive happiness; when you look at others indifferently, you will get the same coldness.

When you have a view different from others, don't doubt yourself or be arrogant. It is admirable to express your real thoughts and communicate sincerely.

If you want to leave a perfect impression on someone, the first step is to smile and remember his or her name.

Some trouble is created by people themselves. And the reasons are that they don't know who they are and what they are after. Besides, they always pursue things that are not suitable for them and beyond their reach in their entire life. This is the cause for dissatisfaction.

When your vanity leads you to raise your status or image by using others' fame or title, do prepare a cushion for yourself in advance, so that you won't hurt so much when you fall.

Don't lower your enthusiasm even if what you get in return is coldness. Some people are cold not because they are used to being cold, but because they are afraid of getting hurt. One day, when your enthusiasm is no longer influenced by others' coldness and malicious words, it will be elevated into human love brimming with radiance of reason.

Don't judge others out of your personal prejudice. You may know someone's story, but you may not know what is behind the story; you may hear of people's comments about this someone, but not experienced the struggles they went through; you may know their misfortune, but not experience their pain. Therefore, please treat others nicely and try to understand them because it is also a way to untie and release yourself.

When you have values different from others', don't make them do what you think they should. When the thought of changing others emerges, it is when the others start to resist you.

Sometimes, silence is not an escape but a way to ease some people's obsession and prejudice.

When your heart is full of love, everyone is here to help you and you are here to help everyone else.

The term "garbage person" is given to those who like to put their own frustrations onto others; as in life it is impossible to live without frustration. One who is wise is able to self-adjust and rid oneself of frustrations. On the other hand, those who throw their mental and emotional baggage onto others not only do not solve their own problems, but cause issues for others. We should strive to be wise, and steer clear of "garbage people".

Those who like you will often see all of your features as positive attributes. Whereas those who do not like you will emphasize your flaws.

Showing warmth to someone who understands gratitude will go a long way. Though sometimes when giving warmth to a cold or selfish person, not only will they not be thankful, but they might also think you have other motives. So be selective with whom you help.

In the process of growing up, you should learn how to be thankful for all those who come into your life, for they have helped create the present and future you.

When people treat you with sincerity, please do not intentionally show off. Showing off will not put you on a higher level, but will in fact put you down.

Never overshare details about yourself with people you are not too familiar with. This oversharing will yield little benefit. It might be that a seemingly harmless or good willed sentence might create hatred in the other. Frustrations or obstacles that originally did not have to exist will start to appear.

Learning from the growth of others is a good thing, but in the

process of doing so do not lose yourself.

As a person, you should be straightforward and honest without undermining other people. Every time you undermine others, your blessings are reduced.

Do not over do it covering your own mistakes. Doing so, you are unknowingly selling out and moving away from your true self.

No matter how high you climb, you can never be taller than the sky. Perching at a high position, you should not look down upon those who have a lower social status. Try your best to create opportunities for them to climb. Only by doing so can your soul appear as honorable as your position.

The good will, when forced upon others, can put pressure on others. If you can change this good will with understanding and respect, the others will accept easily.

Do not be jealous of others' apparent happiness. Perhaps the others may not be as happy as you for some aspects of life. People are used to exhibiting what is good, but endure silently the intangible or tangible pressure themselves.

Some say that those you can not wake up are people who aren't fast asleep, but rather who pretend to be asleep. For those pretenders, first you need to see if there is any necessity to wake them up. If not, then lock them in the room until they could not pretend any more. Or, lie down next to them and pretend to sleep with them until they wake up.

Giving presents among friends is a courtesy. If you are giving a present, then give the best you could afford. Be sure not to give any expired food item or daily necessity. It could damage the friendship because of your carelessness in making such a mistake.

Narrow-minded people like to complain and blame others.

They can even think that everyone else is against them. Broad-minded people do not complain and worry about gains and losses. A broad-mind with no attachment brings peace and serenity.

Do not stare at the fruit of other people's labor, but learn to understand the labor. As the saying goes, a noble person is not greedy for other's nurishment while a narrow-minded person takes away other's acheivements.

The reality is not the reality; all is bound by causality. The truth that people seek is a reflection of the inner attachments and ideals. Behind any truth, in fact, lies a multitude of truths. All these truths are nothing but an excuse to persuade you. Why then do you painstakingly seek that truth?

No matter how much you love, and how much effort you make, if the way you love is not accepted by others, it is time to reflect. Love is mutual, not one-sided and forced.

Life is impermanent. Adapting to changes any time, and one will not be abandoned by the changes.

The best way to stay far from having resentment is be disciplined with oneself and be lenient with others.

Getting more than giving, one will become "ill". Giving without getting, "illness" will decrease.

Those who truly do kind deeds never brag, but spread love silently.

A person's ability does not come from bragging but from action.

Competition in the same trade stimulates awareness of top quality and the improvement of product quality. Therefore, wise people always praise and learn from competitors. Stupid people, in addition to crowding out and slandering competitors, can also cause trouble for them.

All phenomena in the world have both a reality and a false reality. Your thoughts, no matter real or false, can be felt by that, which you are thinking of.

Without virtue, all capability one possesses will turn into nothing. With cultivation of virtue, everything one does will be smooth and auspicious.

Let go of prejudice against others, and treat others with the right views. When you stop being attached to others' mistakes, you will lose the burden of negativity in your heart.

Keep it simple, it becomes easy. Keep it complex, it turns difficult. Stay in the middle, not going to the sides.

Do not see others with a critical eye, for this is what jealousy is. Being critical of others does not raise your status; on the contrary, it helps others to become tolerant.

That you are employable shows your value to others; that you know how to employ others proves your wisdom. The world does not lack workers, but lacks those who can wisely lead others to do good deeds and be good people.

Be a person at ease. Neither compromise out of the consideration of general interests, nor swollen insult and humiliation silently. Do not be a social climber or put on an air of cheerfulness.

If you are abandoned by others, it shows they do not have foresight. If you then abandon yourself, you prove the other to have foresight.

Do not praise your own merits, nor blame others' shortcomings. Merits and shortcomings are two sides of the same thing. It is true for you, and for others too.

Your happiness brings happiness to others. Your sadness brings sadness to others. Emotions determine your environments, which in turn determines healthy, which in turn determines life.

Only truly understand what yielding to others is can one possess the wisdom to do things without indecision.

Yearning for social interaction reflects the inner loneliness. The lonelier it is, the more social interaction is sought after. The social interaction, however, is not the antidote to loneliness. Only by forgiving oneself can one truly understand themselves. Only by knowing to benefit others can one rid the source of loneliness.

Thinking over can be good, but not over thinking.

When applied to the right target, a heart intention can turn into good deeds. When given to those in need, the good deeds bring out the good person.

As an individual, you will never be above nature. Tolerant others in the same way that nature tolerates human beings.

Everyone has their secret. This secret is the bottom line that cannot be invaded. Therefore, if you do not wish to lose others, do not find out their secrets and invade their bottom line.

If you can see others' merits, others will see your wisdom. If you discover others' demerits, others will see your stupidity.

To Simplify a complex problem is wisdom. To make a simple problem complex is stupidity.

One must have the capacity to be tolerant, but not the heart for connivance.

If your kindness is being wrongfully rejected, please do not mind nor complain. Perhaps, that is because you lacked the way to apply wisdom while doing good deeds.

With an understanding of gratitude, love can be a virtuous circle.

A promise should not be changed lightly. If you change your promise because of selfish desire, the selfish desires will change your entire life.

There is a kind of love that does not need words to be understood. With a pure heart and without selfish interests, the love and friendship will last forever.

When you ask what your parents can do for you, ask yourself first what you did for your parents?

The saddest thing one can experience is to deliberately cover up one's mistake with hypocrisy when clearly knowing it is one's mistake.

Persevere doing the right thing, and one day you will see a different you.

A praise is effortless but can produce unimaginable encouragement to those being praised. When you learn to praise others, you have developed a merit for yourself.

No need to refuse a sincere gratitude from someone who has benefited from your help. If you have no intention to show gratitude, do not ask for demands.

Treasure those who are worthy, and you will strengthen the feeling of happiness. Not to be attached to those unworthy, you will reside your vexations.

Self-righteousness leads to stagnation. Let go of pretension, stride ahead and look far, and you will discover more beauty in the wide world.

People who are accustomed to saving other's faces will solve problems easily when they encounter them.

Express your love by actions rather with fancy words, because true love lies in the subtleties.

Don't habitually turn promises to a catchphrase. A promise

without fulfillment is a show of "untrustworthiness".

To overpower is a disease. If not noticed early and self treated, it will make the patient lose themselves in the pain caused by the disease.

Should you stick to your true self, you won't turn into someone you yourself do not even recognize.

Don't comment casually if you don't really understand others' intentions. Make your comments only when you can see the entire situation and understand others.

Even though the saying goes "the hand giving others a rose smells fragrant", you must possess the rose first before handing it to others.

A wise man does not examine others' fault through a telescope, but uses a magnifying glass to observe their own.

Deceiving others is cunning; deceiving oneself is stupid. Therefore one must be honest to themselves, neither deceiving others nor deceiving themselves.

The wise never indulge in exaggeration in verbiage. The wisest words are smiles. Those who are to be great are low-key simple, not impudent and showing off.

Do not teach others what you deemed as truth. Do not constrain yourself by what others consider a principle. Because you are not with the Dao, you cannot understand the truth. Think from others' point of view, think and discern diligently, and you will understand the truth.

If the mind is not broad enough, it is difficult to tolerate others. If a small matter cannot be tolerated, grave disaster is sure to breed.

Everyone longs for a free life, especially those who dislike following outdated rules. However, absolute freedom does not exist. Only when you let go of attachments and desires can you truly achieve spiritual freedom.

Those who give sincerity do not seek anything in return. Those who display false affection often possess other purposes.

The more scared of losing, the more difficult to receive. The happier in giving, the more in receiving.

Overly seeking material gain, one will be controlled by it. Overly being radical, one will have obstacles born out of extremes.

Others know your intentions clearly. They simply do not reveal.

All phenomena have birth and death. The only difference is the length of time in between. Therefore accord with conditions for everything and do not go against them.

Not making conjectures of others casually is the basic cultivation of a person. You are not the other person, and thus you can not truly understand their lives and emotions. Perhaps what you deemed as happiness is worth nothing to them, and perhaps what you consider to be painful is something they gladly endure.

See yourself clearly, and most likely you can see others clearly and get rid of your worries. See others clearly, but you may not see yourself clearly and know what being in the moment is.

Those who are accustomed to letting others get out of an embarrassing situation travel an impeded road in life.

To gain others' trust, be a trustworthy person first. Do remember that not keeping your words for even once will ruin all your credibility。

Do not judge others according to your own standards. Do not use others' requirements to make excessive demand of yourself. Each person's own conditions are different, and thus the ways and standards of doing things also differ.

Do not think an altruistic deed is not worth doing when it is as easy to do as lifting a finger just because there is no gain. Do not seek personal gain at public expenses just because of the craving for a moment of gain.

True love is selfless. Fake love is filled with desires. Do not engage in selfish deeds under the name of love; do not use a selfish heart to confuse true love.

Those who like to find excuses for their mistakes will, sooner or later, lose their true selves because of their mistakes.

Do not rush to talk if your thinking is only surface deep. Remaining silent will allow you to see the truth of the matter.

Good wishes may not come true, but negative worries can become real if they are talked about again and again. Send good wishes more and worry less in life.

Live with worries, and worries will be countless. Live with happiness, and happiness is boundless.

Those who regarded themselves as outstanding are often limited by their views and knowledge. The truly outstanding people can always discover or find those who are even more outstanding than them and constantly make strides and grow.

As long as your heart is grateful, you will often encounter good affinity. Conversely, evil affinity is constant until the heart understands this.

Tolerance is cultivation. Indulging is ignorance.

Those who can speak the truth with you may not necessarily be your family members, but they are someone who should be treasured.

Not adept at fighting off wandering thoughts and desires, one has difficulty embarking on a bright and correct life path.

If you cannot touch the one you redeemed important with your true heart, change your true heart to no intention, and perhaps you will have some unexpected gain.

A truly capable person is not arrogant, but modest.

Those who are able to control their emotions can take initiatives; those who cannot are doomed to be passive.

There are no ifs and buts in life. No need to regret over past deeds because everything is the best arrangement regardless of the results.

Do not complain that the environment is unfit for growth. True talent can unleash the potential to its fullest anywhere.

If you are slandered without any fault of your own, please stay calm. Innocence does not need to be over-explained to others.

The loving-kindness that is being self-promoted is not the real kind because the real kind does not need praise.

Those who put themselves in others' shoes understand others. Those who examine an issue from their own point of view can only see other's shortcomings, not theirs.

Those who constantly complain about bad luck must reflect on this behavior. The moment one decides to change such behavior and let kind thoughts rise is the day good luck emerges.

Loving someone is not lip service. It is turning love into motivation to doing every small thing in life and touching the loved one with your innermost sincerity and caring.

You cannot decide on your birth; however, you can decide what kind of person you will grow to be.

Kind thoughts any time brings auspicious affinities in your surroundings.

Do not force others to accept what they do not need. Giving others what they want the most demonstrates cultivation and wisdom.

Sharing your loving kindness with kind people does not mean you discriminate. Rather, such a choice makes you stay far from those who are unkind.

It is not fearful that one has shortcomings and illness. What is frightening is the disappearance of the moral bottom line and the sense of responsibility.

A high-quality life does not necessarily only belong to those with economic means. It is easier for those who are content with a simple and frugal life to achieve such a life.

Simplicity and frugality is a habit and a spirit too. When your life becomes simpler and more frugal, you will find the truth of life.

What happens during the day appears to be real until it disappears like the clouds. What happens in a night dream seems fake yet real. Real or not, all is a dream. Nothing is worth your attachment.

Do not utter mean words when speaking because doing so brings bad luck to yourself. Do not fill to the rim when pouring water because doing so will make the water overflow.

Nourishing the child with materialism and satisfying their materialist demands, you will only raise a child with no concept of money, no understanding of self-struggle and relying solely on the parents.

The strength of one single person is small. Many people together can ignite a magnificent fire if everyone throws in a firewood. The word "crowd" thus explains the relativity of big and small in life.

第四章

工作事业篇 / Work and Career

飛燕迎風

成功人士普遍具备一个优点，就是发现错误能马上改正，永远不会替自己的错误找理由。

为了保住自己手中的权力而千方百计地排挤他人的人，也许会因此保住一时的地位，却不知已经减损了德行。

经常把职场规矩挂在嘴边的人，往往最不遵守职场规矩。你不必浪费精力去判断这类人的言行对错，只须尽自己本分，留意不给对方落井下石的机会。

生活中，有些顺缘不一定是顺缘，只是很多人没有发现而已。因此当你运气特别好的时候，一定不要得意忘形，要心生警惕，同时为坏运气的出现做好准备。

一个人的成长和改变，需要时间和阅历，而不是接受过多少填鸭式的教导。当你步入该成长的节点时，也许某个灵感或契机会让你醍醐灌顶、振聋发聩，瞬间发生惊人变化。

做成事的基础是自己首先要有自信，但千万不能在自信中尝到一点甜头就轻视他人。唯有在自信里懂得谦虚和尊重他人的人，才不会因为自满招致失败。

当你对某个领域的知识还不精通时，请不要在众人面前畅谈你自己的观点。因为你的观点非但得不到大家的认可，还降低了大家对你的认识和评价。

要想改变世界，必须从改变自己的心灵开始。

撬动世界的最佳支点不是地球、不是国家，也不是别人，而是自己的心灵。

不要因别人的怕苦、怕累退出某项工作而动摇自己的信念，遇到困难而中途退出者，将无法与你共享成功的喜悦。坚持走下去，也许在物质上不会有很多收获，但成长经历将成为生活给予你的最大回报！

无论工作还是生活，都要松弛有度。不要因为拼搏、奋斗的忙碌而忽略内心的从容与安乐。

休假、休闲要讲究松弛有度，那些影响身心、不利于健康的过度的娱乐不但不会让你身心放松，反而会给自己和亲人增添无谓的烦恼和负担。

善于把有效的资源合理运用，达到共赢是智慧，放着资源舍不得利用纯属浪费。

靠别人的声望来抬高自己的人，终究会因借势不利而摔跤。

没有智慧却想谋划大事的人，所做之事不易成功。内心不善，却想谋求长远者一定很难如愿。

才能出众者一定不是最有智慧的，因为有智慧的人不会轻易显露自己的才能。

不要羡慕别人现在的成功，也不要陶醉自己曾经的辉煌。只有活在当下，擦亮自己的心智，看清本我，才会明白自己最需要什么。

凤凰只有经过涅槃才能获得重生。人只有经过挫折才会成熟。

当你在人生某个阶段成功时，请一定不要忘记感恩曾经帮助过你的人。当你在人生某个阶段失败时，一定不要记恨曾经导致你跌入低谷的人。

你在老板眼里的价值，不仅是做事时的认真态度，还有你遇事后的承担精神。

领导用人，很少因对方名气大而选拔，关键是要看候选人的真实能力是否能胜任所需要的工作岗位。

不要只看大事而忽略小事，往往小事可以变成巨大的动力，为你的事业推波助澜。

人们常常会花长时间来规划未来的生活和伟大的目标，但不知有时候那不经意的细节，会让事情有所改变，唯在重要时刻才能看到有价值的小事的力量。

不要迷恋成功，也不要执着失败。脚踏实地，活在当下，做好自己该做的每一件事情，成功就在不远前方。反之，你将步入失败的轨道。

你每天都像陀螺一样不停地忙着旋转，几乎没有留意生活中美丽的风景，以至于自己几乎忘却了年少时的梦想，忘记了生活中除了工作和财富，还有家庭、健康、快乐、朋友等。如果你把工作和财富当成了生活的全部，那你就会错过沿途太多的风景。

昨天所取得的任何成就或者荣誉，都已写入你人生的旅途，成为了过往的历史。唯有当下取得的辉煌，才足以证明你存在的价值。

不管你的本领是与生俱来的，还是后天习得

的，当你不为社会大众服务或开始损人利己时，你身上所具备的能力和本领一定会随之失去。

你用十分的能力去做八分的事情，一定游刃有余，如果你用八分的能力去做十分的事情，一定会非常吃力。因此，轻易不要跟别人争抢做自己不擅长的事情。

不要认为马路有清洁工打扫，就可以随地乱扔垃圾；不要认为宾馆有服务员清理，就可以把房间物品弄乱；不要认为独处时言行不受约束，就去逾越道德底线。坚守准则，做更好的自己。

费尽心思把明天的计划讲得多好听，都赶不上“变化”二字。最好不要到处炫耀不切实际的空想，那只是你的计划而非现实。

成功的人习惯记住别人的优点，忘掉别人的缺点。难于成功的人却习惯把抱怨挂嘴边，他人缺点常记心间。

你是否勤于回顾和总结过往？过去的事情，无论成败都已定格，重要的是我们从这些或远或近的历史中学习和收获了什么，善于总结和怀想才能继往开来！

成功的经验不是来自培训，而是来自你一次次失败的积累。仔细观察，不难发现那些容易被洗脑的人，都是不愿意下功夫走正路，千方百计找捷径的人。所以说，成功的企业家里没有一个接受过成功学的培训，而热衷于成功学培训的人，没有一个能成为真正的企业家。

衡量一个人或一个团体的能量（或价值）的大小，最简单的标准就是看它肩上承载家国责任的大与小和对正义的担当！

真正有内涵的作品，必须经得起历史的考验和众人的评判。

办事要分轻重缓急，不能意气用事。如重视小的而忽视大的，把后办的事情先办，先办的事情后办，会扰乱做事的程序。

真心为国家和人民做事的人，所做的事情是不受时间和空间限制的。也许，这就是你工作、生活诸事百顺的原因。

若真正能明白名誉、地位如梦如幻，你就不会在意或执着做事的成败与得失。

做下级的如果心怀畏惧而不敢讲真话，做上级的如果心怀骄傲只爱听美言，那么上级所听到的只会是一些虚假情况。在这样的状态中去做事，绝难成功。

固然你有日行千里的本领，但也必须和常人一样先迈出一只脚才开始前行。也许你具备做大事的能力，但也要从小事做起。

如果你不自量力地去做自己难于把握的事情，

就好比孩童背巨石，将会自讨苦吃。

内心阳光，做事才会坦荡。

做领导身边的工作人员，一定不要阻挠正直的人为领导提供合理化建议和意见。做领导者不能只爱听他人的称颂，而不接受直谏。

你若不想做的事儿，就别给自己找不去做的借口或给他人找去做的理由；你若想做别人正在做的事儿，也别故意挑剔他人方法不当或能力不够。因为这并不是凸显你“能力”的最佳方式。

不要懊恼自己的努力白白为他人做了嫁衣，其实你是在为自己储备力量。因此，我们要做事就要做到最好。

每个有良知的医生都愿意恪守医德，尽力治愈或减轻病患的痛苦。有些未尽人意的情形，尚因人类技术所限和存在未知，因此要理解医者之无助。

能成大事者，不在于有无权势，而是能不能遵纪守法、洁身自爱，严格要求自己。能让人心服者，不在于此人是否会讲甜言蜜语，而是能不能做到言行一致，以诚待人。

无论你成功与否，请记着给自己的心灵找一个归属。因为人生最大的痛苦就是心灵没有归属感。

世间没有所谓可适合所有人和所有情况的生活秘笈，你每天从外界及他人身上学到的知识与智能，只是为增强你更好实现自我的功力而已。学习知识和挖掘自己同样重要。

别人的成功你永远无法复制，因为别人的成功学来自他们本身的特质，外加当时的各种因素的综合影响以及他们的不懈努力，等等，照搬硬套也不能变成你的成功宝典。成功是一种取决于各种因素的“私人定制”。

不求有功、但求无过的思想虽然能保全自己，但实质上是阻碍发展与进步的负能量，是负国负民之大错，因为无功即有过也。

当我们有缘遇到有德行的老师时，请不要像对待普通朋友那样让时间虚度，而是应该向老师虚心学习。千万别错过讨教解决问题的最佳机会。

无论您做的事情有多么正确，都会有不同意见出现。此时，既不能因多人支持而傲慢，也不要因出现不同意见而气馁。不为利，不失己利。

从失败中获得感悟之时，即是你走向成功之日。

一个内心充满爱、身上散发正能量的人，就像金色阳光涌入，既照亮了周围的人，也温暖了自己。爱心人人都有，只要你无私给予、不求回报，大爱就会和金色阳光一样相互温暖和传递。

言行一致是立身做人的根本，是踏实做事的基础。

善于解决问题的人，在事业上一定会超越事事找借口的人。

有远见的人，一定会比只懂得完成今天计划的人得到更多的机遇。有全局观的人一定会比只注重个人得失的人拥有更大的胸怀！

成熟且自信的人，不会把心思花在取悦和亲附别人上，而是会将更多精力投入在提升和修炼自己方面。如果你是大海，百川自来汇聚。自信与自强才是坚固的柱石！

用心工作的人，终有一日会成为那些应付上班人的领导，也将成为工作和生活的主人。

生活中，想大有作为的人很多，但是真正愿意

把小事做好、大事做实的人却不多。无论公益还是慈善都需要从小事做起，从实事做起，汇聚众人之力必能成功。

多学点本领是有用的，因为没有人会帮你一辈子，至少你要学一个为自己生存创造条件的本领。

人到晚年，你能留住的不是金钱、地位和权力，而是人生中最美好的回忆。因此，从年轻开始就不要考虑为自己留下什么，而是为祖国、社会和人民留下什么。

走在人生路上，你会遇到很多的十字路口。此时，不是你给别人引路，就是别人给你指路。切记：如果你想给别人引路，首先自己要知道路怎么走；如果你不知道对方问的路怎么走，请勿随意指路。因为今天你给别人引错了路，明天别人也会为你或他人指错路。

在成长的路上，能打开心灵的那把钥匙不是别

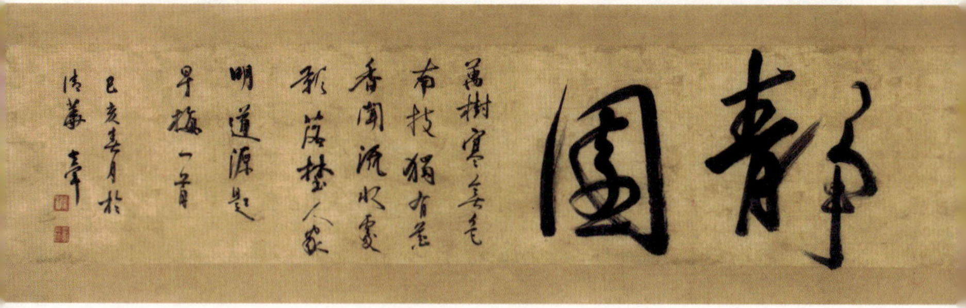

人而是自己。很多时候，心灵所需要的不是建议、教导、方法，而是温暖的阳光。

在生活与工作中，当你遇到进退两难，不知如何抉择时，千万不要逃避，不妨退而求其次。做好最坏的打算，往往会让你否极泰来，旗开得胜。

如果有一天遭遇了墙倒众人推的境遇，请告诫自己，能让你倒下的只有自己，那些想推倒你的人，都是让你倍加坚强的助力源。

成熟的人不会因为不喜欢工作中的某个人而影响工作态度或效率。

生活就是修行，不要迷信外力。一次做好一件事，效率要高于同时想做很多事。其实在你思考的同时，别人已经做完了你正在思考的事情。

真朋友交往没有太多华丽的语言，遇到事情才会显出无私奉献的友谊。

在精神层面上超越了周围的人时，就意味着将要忍受常人精神之外的孤独。这不是真正意味的孤独，而是内心世界的升华。

人有喜欢走捷径的本能，但人生的路没有捷径可走。唯脚踏实地的走过一个又一个经历，才能不断成长。

所有的成功都离不开坚持，能把一件事坚持到最后的人，终将成就自己的愿望。

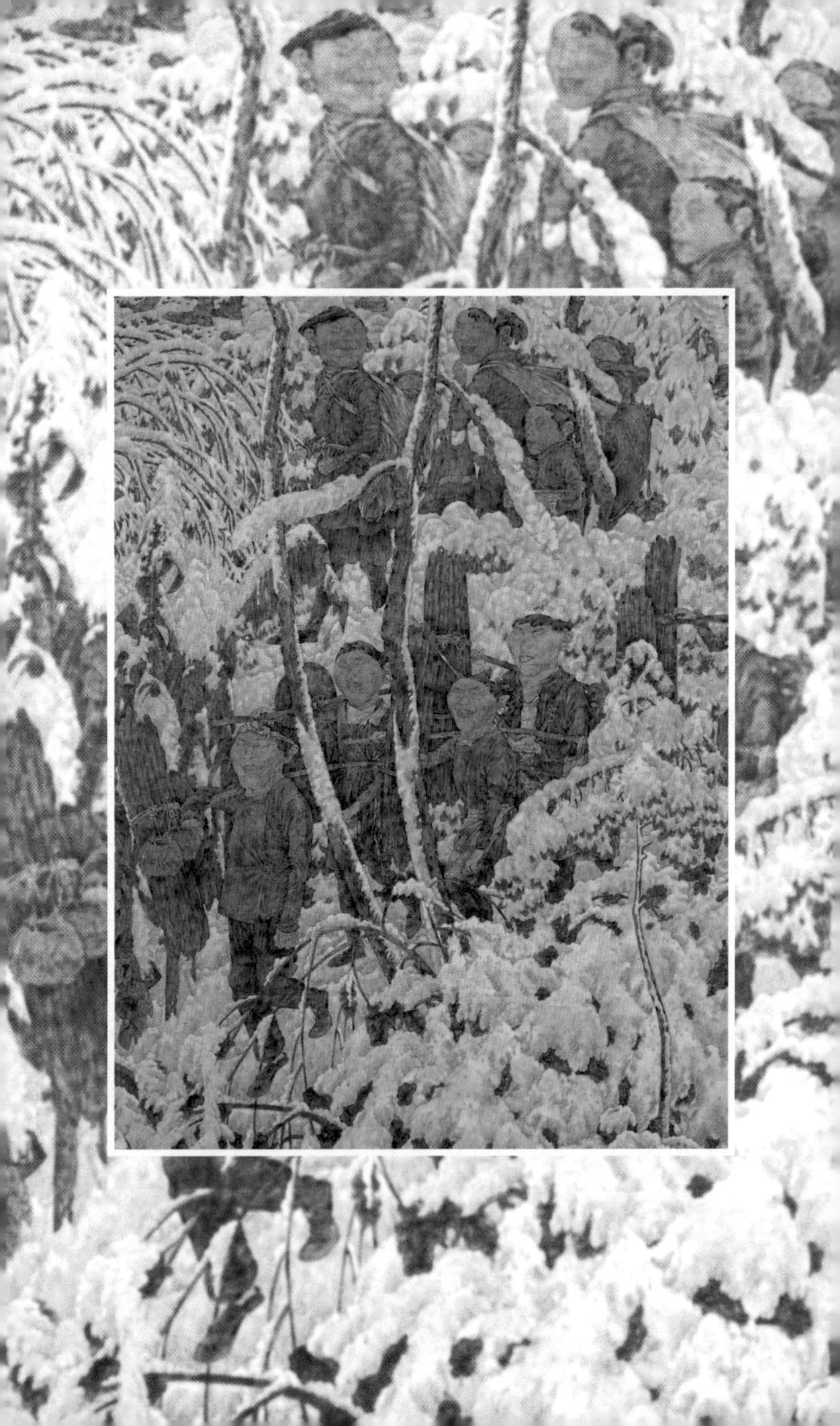

All successful people share a common merit: revise errors immediately and never find any excuses.

In order to protect his own power and do everything possible to exclude others, he may therefore maintain a position for now, but his virtue has been tarnished.

He who always talks about the workplace rules is often the last to follow those rules. You don't need to waste time to judge their words and actions. All you need to do is perform your own duty and give them no chance to frame you.

"Good luck" may not lead to a good ending, but most of the people don't realize this. So when you are in your good times, don't be carried away; instead, be cautions and get ready for your fortunes to turn.

Only time and experience, rather than cramming instructions, can endow a person with maturity. When you get to this turning point, perhaps a flash of inspiration or an opportunity will fill you with wisdom. Therefore, you may make astonishing changes.

The basis of success is confidence, but you can never look down upon others after tasting the sweetness of confidence. Only those who know modesty and respect of others while keeping self-confidence can avoid failure resulting from complacency.

When you are not proficient in a certain field, you should better not boast about your viewpoints in front of people. If you do boast, your opinion will not get anyone's approval; on the contrary, it lowers other's views of you.

To change the world, one must begin with oneself. The best fulcrum to move the world is not the earth, the countries nor other people, but one's own heart.

Don't be discouraged when other people drop out of certain work because of the hard-work and endurance required. Those people cannot share the joy of success with you. Keep going even if you may not have a lot of material gains; the experience will become the greatest reward!

Try to be balanced in both your work and your life. Do not ignore your own happiness because of hard work.

Vacation and leisure should be balanced too. Excessive unhealthy entertainment can't relax your soul. On the contrary it burdens yourself and loved ones with unnecessary worries and troubles.

Utilizing the resources in a reasonable way and achieving a win-win situation is wisdom; saving the resources without using them is a waste.

He who raises himself by relying on others' fame will eventually fall over because of the unfavorable occasion.

He who is of great ambition yet without wisdom will not easily succeed. He who is seeking long-term success without a kind heart will encounter many difficulties.

Talented people may not be the wisest since the latter will not easily reveal their talent.

Don't envy other people's success and don't be intoxicated in your past achievements. Only by living in the moment, opening your mind and knowing your true self can you understand what you need the most.

Phoenix can only be reborn after nirvana. A man can only be mature after going through setbacks.

When you succeed at a certain stage of your life, you should be grateful to those who have helped you. When you failed at some point in your life, you must not bear grudges against the people who drove you to that.

How your boss values you depends not only on your attitude but also your commitment to the team.

When selecting the person for a job, the leaders rarely make the selection based on the person's fame only. The key is to see whether the candidate's ability can meet the requirements of the job.

You should not only focus on the big things and ignore the trivial ones, which usually would add impetus to

your career. People would spend much time planning for the big goals of the future, but they may not understand that the trivial details can sometimes change things greatly. Only when it comes to the critical moment can they see the value of trivial things.

Don't be infatuated with success, and don't be attached to failure either. Live in the moment and do everything you need to do well, and success is right ahead of you. If you do not, you have already stepped on the path for failure.

You keep yourself so busy every day that you nearly have any time to enjoy the beautiful scenery along the way. Soon you will forget your dreams from childhood, and forget the importance of health, happiness, family, and friends. If you only bear work and wealth in your mind, you would miss too many beautiful sceneries in life's journey.

The accomplishments or honors from yesterday have all been written into your life journey and became a history. Only the achievements now can prove the value of your existence.

Regardless your capabilities are innate or learned, you have to serve the public. When you start harming others for your own benefit, you will lose your ability and skills.

You will feel that you can handle it easily if you are more than equal to a task, and you will feel tough if you are less than equal to the task. So make sure that you don't fight others to do what you are not good at.

Don't take a street cleaners' job for granted and throw out garbage anywhere you want; don't take a hotel housekeepers' job for granted and mess up your room; and do not think that you need not take responsibility for your speech and behavior when you are alone and cross the bottom line of morality. Stick to moral standards and be a better you.

No matter how beautifully you articulated your future plans, changes will always happen. So, you'd better not show off an unrealistic dream since it's just a plan rather than the reality.

Successful people tend to remember the good of others and forget their shortcomings. The unsuccessful ones are used to complaining about others and keeping other's shortcomings in mind.

Do you reflect on your past often? Whether it is a success or a failure, what happened in the past belongs to the past. What is more important is to learn from the past and draw lessons from the experience. Reflecting can ensure you a better future!

You can only gain experience accumulated from each failure other than from training. Take a good look and you will find that those who can be easily brainwashed are not willing to work hard but want a shortcut to success. So it can be said that no successful entrepreneurs have ever taken any training on how to succeed, and those who are keen on the training can never become a real entrepreneur.

The simplest way to determine how valuable a person or a group of people could be is to measure how much responsibility and righteousness they shoulder!

A masterpiece must withstand the test of history and the judgement of the public.

Things should be taken up in order of priority not by personal feelings. It is difficult to do a good job if you do it in the wrong order.

People who have devoted themselves to their country and their people will not be limited by time and space. Perhaps this is why their work and life are so smooth.

If you can really understand that reputation and power are not the real thing, then you won't care too much about success or failure.

If the subordinates fear to tell the truth and the supervisors only like to listen to good words, then the supervisors can only get false information. In this way, they will never succeed.

Even if you have talent, you still must lift a foot up first in order to take a step, just like any ordinary person does. You perhaps have the ability to make great achievements, but you still need to start from the trivial things.

If you go beyond your own depth, you are asking for troubles like a child tries to carry a heavy rock on the back.

Only when your heart is full of sunshine can you be open-hearted.

Working closely beside the leader of your organization, you should never stop an upright man from providing reasonable suggestions and advice to your leader. As a leader, one cannot just listen to praise but reject unpalatable advice.

If you don't want to do one thing, do not give yourself excuses not to do it or find reasons for others to do it. If you want to do what others are doing, you should not be deliberately picky about other people's method or incapability because it's not the best way to show your "ability".

Your efforts may have done good for others but may not for yourself. Do not be discouraged. You actually build up your own reserves through your efforts. Therefore, whatever we do, we should always give our best shot.

Every conscientious doctor is willing to follow the medical ethics and do their best to eliminate or alleviate the suffering of a patient. Some unpleasant endings are due to limitations of technology. Thus, we should understand that the medical workers cannot do everything.

He who is able to make great accomplishments will observe discipline, keep his integrity and is strict with himself. You can never make people sincerely convinced with your words of honey. Only when you live up to your words and treat people with sincerity can you make them convinced of you.

Whether you are successful or not, please remember to find your heart a home because the greatest pain in life is that you can't feel a sense of belongings from the bottom of your heart.

There is no such a secret method that can suit everyone and every situation; the knowledge and intelligence you learn from the outside world is to enhance your ability to realize yourself. Exploring oneself is as important as learning knowledge.

You can never copy others' success because they succeed in their own way. The successes are determined by various factors such as personal traits, the situation and efforts. Influenced by various factors, success is customized.

"Not aspire to be meritorious but only to be blameless." This kind of thinking can protect one from being blamed but it is actually a negative energy that will hinder the development and progress of the country, because no contribution is indeed a mistake in itself.

When you are destined to meet a teacher with virtue and

morality, you should cherish the time and learn from your teacher modestly. Do not miss this best opportunity to learn.

No matter how right you think what you are doing is, there will always be a different opinion. You can't be arrogant for the support of the majority; and you can't be discouraged because someone disagrees with you. When you are not after self-interest, you will actually not lose your own benefits.

The moment you realize the true meaning of a failure is the beginning for you to succeed.

A person with a heart full of love and a body full of energy is like a ray of golden sunshine illuminating himself and the people around. Everyone has love. As long as you give selflessly and don't ask for return, love will be passed on just like the golden sunshine.

Consistent words and deeds are the foundation of being a decent human being. This is the way one conducts oneself in society.

People who are good at solving problems will go further in their career than those who always make excuses.

People of vision can get more opportunities than people who will only accomplish due tasks. People who have an overall view will be more broad-minded than those who only focus on personal gains and losses!

People who are mature and confident won't waste time in pleasing others; rather, they focus on bettering and cultivating themselves. If you are the sea, all rivers will run into you. Confidence and strength are your strong cornerstones!

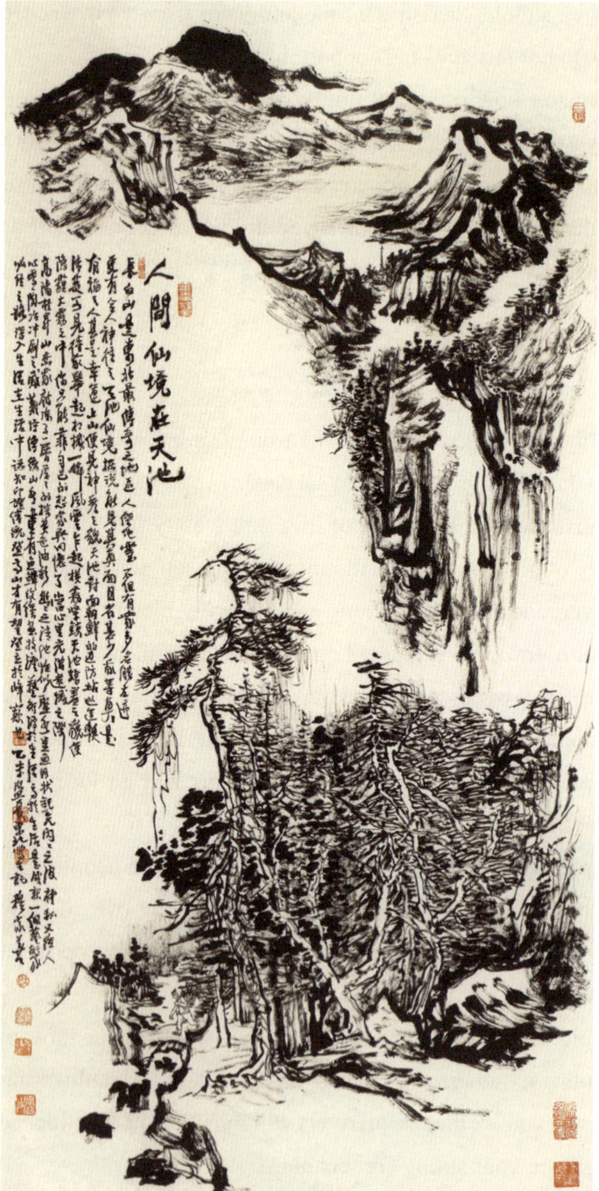
人間仙境在天池

People who work hard will be the leaders of those who hardly work and will become the masters of their work and life.

In life, many people want to do great things, but only a few are willing to do small things and do them well. Whether it is public welfare or charity, you should start from small and practical things. Gathering the strength of the many will lead you to success.

It is useful to learn more skills because no one will help you forever. You should at least learn some survival skills.

When you are old, what you can keep is not money, status or power, but the best memories of your life. Therefore, when you are young, do not ponder what you can keep for yourself when you are old, but think what contributions you can make for your country, the society and people.

You will encounter a lot of crossroads in your lifetime and don't know which way to go. At that point, you either give advice or take it from others. Remember to only point the direction to others when you know where to go. Otherwise, you should better not give others advice. If you show them the wrong way today, tomorrow you may be led to a wrong way too.

As you grow, the key to opening your soul is not someone else but yourself. Often what the soul needs is not advice, instructions or methods, but the warmth of the sunshine.

In life or work, when you encounter a dilemma and do not know how to make a choice, be sure not to escape. You might as well take a step back and prepare for the worst. Often doing so will bring good fortune out of the worst misfortune and lead you to success.

"When a wall is to collapse, everybody gives it a shove." If someday you run into such a situation, please caution yourself this - The person who can really put you down is no one but yourself; those who want to put you down are the source that makes you extremely strong.

Mature people will not change their attitude toward work and their efficiency just because they do not like someone at work.

Life is cultivation. Do not be superstitious of external forces helping you. Doing one thing well is more efficient than trying to do many things at the same time. In fact, as you are thinking of multitasking, others have already finished what you are thinking about doing.

Superficial and splendid language is not needed among real friends. The true friendship shines with selfless dedication when a situation calls for it.

Surpassing people around you spiritually means you will endure the loneliness that comes with it. This loneliness, however, is not the loneliness in the true sense; rather, it is the sublimation of your inner world.

Enjoying short-cuts in life is a human instinct. However, there are no short-cuts in life. Only through down-to-earth experience one by one can we continue to grow.

All success is inseparable from perseverance. A person who can persevere to the end will eventually fulfill his wish.

第五章

亲情友情篇 / Kinship and Friendship

人不仅要延续父母的血脉，更要传承让你引以为豪的家族精神。

不要打着孝敬父母的说辞去做非法的事情，其实任何一位父母宁可自己受苦，也不愿意儿女用这种方式去尽孝道。

人与人的交流，不只是言语的交流，还有心灵之间的对话。当彼此怀恨的时候，心会相距很远；而彼此心里有爱的时候，心心相印无距离。

在未经朋友允许的情况下，无论什么原因都不宜把朋友的隐私信息告诉他人。如若你这么做了，说明你没把此人当作真正的朋友。

男人的自信来自于女人的鼓励，女人的自信来自于男人的欣赏。

在紧张的生活中偶尔开个小玩笑，也无伤大雅。但是，生活可以轻松，行为却不能轻浮。我们的言谈举止可以轻松自然，但不能放荡轻浮。尤其男女之间，轻浮的举动是对人的不尊重。

都说父母是孩子最好的老师，其实孩子也是父母的老师。因为孩子就像父母的一面镜子，无论父母身上的优点还是缺点，都会在孩子身上表现得一览无余。

如果爱，就告诉她（他），不要以友情的名义去爱着一个人；如果不爱，就以友情的名义去拒绝，这样就不会伤害她（他）。

欣赏一个人无需理由，没有原因。生命中的每个人都是你的过客。有些人与之邂逅，转身忘记；有些人与之擦肩，必然回首，只为欣赏。

女人需要关心和疼爱，但不要仅在过节时才被想起。

亲情、友情和爱情自有定数，请不必因疏远、离弃而难过。已过去的情感是难以追寻的，懊悔和痴迷都不是明智之举。

感恩父母最好的方式不仅是给他们钱物，还要多做一些能让父母开心、以你为荣的善举，不做让父母感到羞耻的事情。

爱他（她）之前，先爱自己，因为爱自己不是自私，而是爱的法则之基。

当你开心过节，与家人幸福团圆时，请不要忘记还有很多人为了祖国大家庭的安康而放弃与家人团聚，坚守在自己的工作岗位上。

当你特别执着于某个人、某件事时，只会感受到短暂的快乐。但到头来，终究是苦大于乐。也许只有过来人，对于爱情的辛酸，才有特别深刻的体会。

为名利而结合的婚姻，终究因贪图虚荣名利而自尝苦果。

男女相交如饮水止渴，要守好道德底线，因为瞬间的爱慕会如同天降白雪遇暖而化。

从古至今，为情所困、为物所迷的人数不胜数。如果你能不为情与物所束缚，在旧物里找到新的启示，在旧情里找到新的智慧，便可进出无碍，打开无限广袤的天空。

当你还没有感受到爱的时候，并不代表你身边没有爱。可能是身边的人表达爱的方式不同。

你受伤害时，并非全部来自他人伤害，或许，是你过于敏感。

何为善友？就是和你交往没有任何功利心，当你遇到困难时会全力帮忙；当你大富大贵了，也不会恭维和巴结；不管你身在何处，有没有权力地位，每逢过年过节，他的祝福都会如约而至。

如果分手无法避免，请你重新调整心情。在旁人无法触及的内心深处藏好，就此

深埋在记忆的深海，不复提起。

两个人如果没有了初恋的激情，请珍惜彼此的感情。当你准备放手的时候，还请你先想想当初为何陪她（他）走到这里。

真正爱你的人，一定不舍得在你最困难的时候离你而去。

夫妻、情侣之间发生争执有时难免，要是发展到家庭暴力，就会深深的伤害对方。无论脾气有多差，都不要伤害对方的身体来发泄不满。

婚姻中真正伤害感情的不是偶尔争执，而是争吵后的冷战。

从早到晚只知道拼命地赚钱、追求利益而少有关爱他人者，真的很可怜。因为他们历经世事风雨，辛苦操劳一生，终究在情义上一无所获。

有一种爱，不是建基于利益、情义和血缘的关系之上，而是超越世俗，达到爱人如己才是真正的爱。

靠吃喝玩乐维系出来的“友谊”，不是真正的

友谊。唯有用心理解、用诚相交、用爱浇灌、用时间施肥、用智慧除草、肝胆相照后的情谊才会盛开友谊之花，缔结友谊之果。

爱你或者不爱你的人，这辈子与你或许只有一次相处的缘份。如不珍惜当下在一起共处的时光，无论爱与不爱，下辈子都不会再相见。

请不要经常把自己曾经为国家和人民、为家庭与亲朋作过的贡献挂在嘴边，更不要和他人炫耀已长、攀比功劳。因为，你所做的是给自己培养福田。居功傲慢的行为，会消耗福报。

相爱易，相处难。因环境和价值观的不同，每个人走进爱情魔方的感觉也各不相同，甘苦滋味只有自己最清楚。

当你在爱情的旅行中感觉疲倦时，请不要改变初心。先静心拷问自己的初心是喜欢远处的那高山雪莲，还是眼前的腊月梅花。

不少人追求爱情的目的大都是为了走向婚姻，可走进婚姻殿堂的人却很难找到梦想中爱情的感觉。

不怕累的女人，是想用工作填满自己的生活，自立自强，不因弱小无助而受伤。

孤独的爱情也许非常凄美感人，但不及一个懂你的人在你最需要时的陪伴。

离别莫伤感，暂时的离别可以增添再次相见的浓郁情深；相逢莫激动，今日的相逢也许是永久的离别。

出现在你生命里的每一个人都是你的缘，无论善缘还是恶缘都要用心去接纳。唯有接纳后的缘才会真正和你了缘，否则总有一天还会有相同的缘出现在你的身边。

纵然用尽一切办法，也无法阻止时光流逝对美人的改变。欣赏女人年轻貌美所洋溢的青春风采，也要品味岁月流转所赋予的成熟美！

与良友相交，不富则贵；和损友相交，不惨则败。

朋友之间可以互利，但不可利用。利用友谊填充私欲沟壑的人永远不可能有真正的知己。

男女之间浪漫爱情的体现不是在公共场所搂搂抱抱、接吻撒娇的亲密表白，而是时刻都考虑和关注如何给彼此精神或者生活创造温馨浪漫的氛围。

无论你有多高的艺术造诣，都不要用作品的价值与友情相提并论。因为当你让作品的价值高于友谊时，众叛亲离已经为期不远。

不要以为男女之爱必须增添性的作料才是真爱，这是为需求和欲望找的理由和借口。真正爱一个人时，不是祈求二人必须有性，而是设身处地的用道德标准去保护和珍爱对方的名节。

婚姻的幸福程度不是他人决定的，而是在于对婚姻的忠诚度和责任感。认为婚姻不幸的人，首先是对婚姻的幸福要求超越了自己的经营范围，其次是计较婚姻中自己付出的多而得到的少，且怀疑另一半对自己的好不是真心。

徒有天使容颜而没有贤良性格，徒有富帅外表而没有责任承当，这样的男神、女神未必是你的人生良伴。

真正的爱，可以超越生命的长度、心灵的宽度、灵魂的深度。关注纯粹的内在品质，而不在意外在的形式和装裱。

感情有浓郁、寡淡之分，亦有长久、短暂之别。灿烂到极致也会燃烧绽放，过后皆成灰烬，欲维持感情的温度，需要持久恒常地投入情感，也需要理性的调控。

在家里孝敬父母的人，到外面才能交到真正的朋友。反之，所交之人很难是善类。

无论多么优秀的男人都有脆弱的一面，不论多么柔弱的女人也有她坚强的地方。因此，我们既要包容优秀男人的那一点脆弱，也要理解柔弱的女人某些方面的强大。

夫妻有报恩、报怨、讨债和还债四种缘份。无论什么缘份让彼此结合，都要珍惜在一起的缘份。因为，无论多么恩爱的夫妻终有离别时。当生命终结，从此永别。

有的人看似和你距离很远，但你落难时他一定不会袖手旁观。当你摆脱困境感谢他时，却发现他已悄悄地走远。这种人，千万不要用金钱去感激他，因为他图的不是你的钱，而是希望你在己所能及的条件下多帮助身边那些需要帮助的人，之后和他们一起把爱传递出去。

外部强力的说教，未必能使一个人从思想上领悟到什么是真正的爱。易仿效的方式，就是我们能像父母无私爱我们那样去爱他人，经过不断的锻炼和尝试，我们所收获的不仅仅是丰盛的爱，还能提高的爱的能力。

俗语称“亲戚分远近，朋友有厚薄”，虽然这句话流传广泛，但却不甚有理。如果凡事以诚相待、没有分别地付出，站在不厚此薄彼的起点，那

么站在终点收获的也会是可期待的情真意挚。

找朋友帮忙，也要学会三思而后行，如果是自己能办妥的事情，就不要麻烦别人；如果是超过朋友能力的事情，也不应期待别人的成全。

错过一辆车，你可以等。错过一个人，也许就是一辈子。遇到一个对你好的人一定要珍惜，否则失去后将不再回来。

分手的爱情好比断了线的风筝，只能让它飞，不要死死抓住曾经那份甜美的回忆不放，放过它便是放过自己。如若纠结于那不开心的爱情，便会落得一季花开，满地忧伤。

以责人之心责己，以恕己之心恕人，误会后的坚冰就会慢慢融化，亲情、友情、爱情也会再次复苏。你在为别人开启一扇窗的同时，也能让自己看到金色的阳光。

一个人对有魅力的异性，产生一时留恋而倾慕对方是很正常的，但不要把心动、留恋或倾慕误以为爱情。殊不知心动的感觉最多只像宝石的光彩，让你惊叹它的精美。而真爱就像阳光，日子久了或许会让你觉得十分平常，但这种光辉和温暖一旦失去，你就会发现整个世界都堕入了黑暗。

知己，就是彼此相知而情谊深切的人。相互尊重、相互欣赏、相互包容……，托付诸多情愫的人，其实何尝不是终生难觅的另一个自己？

有缘相识实属缘分，一定要珍惜。但珍惜不是你一个人的事儿，如果你的热情遭到冷遇，请不必难过。因为所有相识的人里不一定都喜欢你的性格和做事风格，能和你成为朋友的至少是志同道合者。

最坚固的爱情是敬始慎终，或许还有幸成为动人的杰作！

能把你当朋友者一定不会在通讯录里删除你，所有拒绝你看朋友圈的人一定不会把你当朋友。

家里有十个孩子，有九个人都没收入，只有一个人在奋斗，这个人只能更勤劳，才能支撑这个家庭。这种现象对一个家是如此，对整个社会大家庭呢？

纯粹的爱，就是当新鲜、热情、浪漫所有附属统统被拿掉之后，你仍然愿意拥有对方。

高品质的爱，是换位的体谅与恒生的心疼！

爱是一种自愿发生的并与他人的人生紧密相连的奇妙“物质”！

孩子是父母的反光镜，所暴露的任何一个缺点都值得父母去反思。所以当孩子出现问题时，请不要光在孩子身上或学校、教师、社会等方面找原因，而是要先从自身上找答案。孩子出现问题，做父母应注意孩子的感受，多听听孩子的心里话，而不是用自认为永远正确的观点来批评孩子。

爱情是殊途陌路人共同期许甜蜜的催化剂。

真正的相爱是两个生命感性加理性的彼此发现和接受，并欣然面对未来的一种生活选择！

美景皆需用心去欣赏，才能领略其风采；美人则需用心去关爱，才会得到其芳心。

爱情可以把苦涩镶上金边，让相恋的每一个日子闪闪发亮！

真正的友情，不是在你对他（她）有用时才对你好，而是在你没可用价值时还对你好。

娶妻看德不看貌，以貌娶妻，往往会因小失大，后悔终生。

如此倾心地面对着你，不敢

右顾左盼，即使因爱成殇，也不想转身之间即成天涯而错失你！

在你心宇之中，是否还一直留有一片晴空？让自己独自小憩并期待刻骨的爱情，也许永远都没有遇见他。这孤寂的等待，就是爱情的分量！

明星和公众人物的婚姻或爱情模式并不是你的完美参照系，并不具有照搬和效仿的价值。每个婚姻中的主角，都应在婚姻的锅碗瓢盆中寻找到自己最适合的位置，来谱写属于自己家庭生活的华彩乐章。可恰恰有很多人不知道幸福的婚姻来自于彼此背后的坚守和珍惜，而不是不停地更换乐谱。

与诤友析理，可辨是非；与心灵对话，可见真我！

所谓灵魂伴侣，就是与你一起深入探究生命真相的旅伴，欣赏你的独特、叛逆，疼惜你的脆弱、艰难，与你体验和感受所有苦乐悲喜，错也相守，对也相望，彼此坚定、相互维护。他更像客观世界存在的另一个自己，得之，幸之至也！

爱你的人，不一定真正懂你。但懂你的人如果爱你，这样的爱就更可能贴近灵魂！

我们经常犯惯性错误，比如相爱易、相处难的问题。本来想彼此尊重、互相欣赏和宽容，却又不由自主地把对方当成不良情绪的垃圾桶，拼命地挑毛病，口不择言地伤害对方，然后又后悔连连。这种初心与行为的矛盾表现是我们对爱的极度确信又极度不确信导致的。

给你最恰切的爱，不增一分，不减毫厘，悄然无息，红尘相伴，不奢百年托付，但愿彼此默守！

“爱”与“情”的联姻，是彼此用忠诚的勇敢之心，用时常喜悦的快乐之情，全心、全情投入一起的融合品。“爱”与“情”的成功结合，是因为彼此愿意承担因爱情所衍生的所有责任。

玫瑰花不会因身上带刺儿而减弱自身的美丽，女人也不会因为强势和任性嫁不出去。既然你喜欢她的美，就要试着去欣赏和接纳她身上的刺儿。

离开一个地方，如画风景你带不走；错过一个人，他的一切便与你无关。历尽千帆，看破才知有些失去比拥有更踏实。

一个人，每一天浮世清欢；一个人，每一刻享受生命。缘来，人生无憾；缘去，不缠不恋；缘来缘去，写意悲欢。

我一直在寻觅故事里的那个角儿。原来，你不出现故事根本无法开始！

从恋爱到婚姻通常会经历三个阶段：蜜糖阶段，恋爱时期彼此只看优点，缺点也当优点看；对抗阶段，彼此只看缺点，优点视而不见，势均力敌，折磨窒息；成熟阶段，历经痛苦磨合，终于找到适合彼此的相处之道，同时完成自我锤炼和成长，彼此给“爱”真正找到了爱巢。

人生只有在失意之时，才能体会到友情的可贵。你若没有落寞经历，又怎能知晓谁是知心挚友？谁的情浓意暖呢？

总有些话，一直想对你说，却从未说出口。今天，我鼓足勇气告诉你，遇到你是一个美丽的意外，我愿意珍惜你。

爱情永远不会错过，因为爱情的保质期是永远。错过不是错了，也不是过了，因为那根本不算是爱情或者至少不是你的爱情。

男人如山，女人似水，二者不是死敌，应互为表里。你若伟岸雄奇，她也明艳秀丽；她若水软玉温，你可山包海容，这样唇齿相依就是婚姻的最佳生态！

男人是女人的影子，你怎么照他，影子就会变成什么样子；女人是男人的镜子，你怎样对她，都会在她身上全部展现出来。

如果人们的婚姻始于爱情，而非驱利于虚荣和物质，保持爱的纯粹和温度就成为美好的希冀。理想的婚姻是爱情始终的陪伴，是面对岁月的不离不弃。而爱情是两个人的事情，请在风雨兼程中彼此手拉手抵御平淡的流年，请在油盐柴米中别忘了初恋的激情呵护。用心，是保持婚姻幸福的秘诀，今天，你用心了吗？

喜欢与爱存在最实质的区别：喜欢更多地意味占有和得到，而爱却更倾向给予和付出。只有入心的才是爱！

男女的友情与爱情之间是否存在明确边界？二者是否可以相互转化？友情量的积累真的可以变成爱之缠绵？爱情消逝又可否归于友情？其实二者之间真的没有换算公式，但是确实拥有一个共同点，就是需要相互珍惜。劝君不要贪心，莫做愚笨的人，丢了友情，失了爱情，最后变成陌路人。

最长寿的婚姻能维系多久？恐怕长不及百年。如果你恣意挥霍和践踏只会加速它的逝去。当一段婚姻绝尘远离，如果那时你才扼腕叹息，恐怕已回天乏力！

珍惜今天吧！也许，明天我们再难相逢。

一见钟情是朵彼此倾慕的火花，能否燃成燎原的爱火，还要看有无缘分和足够挚诚！

你欲诉，有人懂。温暖知心的话儿说给相宜相悦的人听，即使天涯也咫尺！

思念滋味的有两种:一种是甜的，还有一种苦的。

婚姻既不是爱情的坟墓，也不是万能灵药。不可期望用婚姻改变爱情，只能期望用爱情来医治婚姻。

结婚是缘于彼此欣赏和相爱，离婚是缘于相爱但不能彼此包容。

女人的美千姿百态，但是最动人的特质却是

温良，拥有这样特质的女人犹如一片平湖，热爱生活，对爱安然静守！

孝道与感恩不只是老祖宗传承下来的文化符号，还是与每个人的工作、生活都息息相关的一种生活习惯。当把这种生活习惯传递和延续的时候，大孝、中孝、小孝就会因感恩而汇集成孝道。

天天捧着你的人不一定是爱你的人，当你无法给予时，一定是最先离你而去的人。偶尔会指出你缺点的人不一定是不爱你的人，当你遇到困境时一定是第一个站出来帮你的人。

人生的美丽，不在于争，而在于守。婚姻又何尝不是！

你对孩子的种种要求并不能培养出他最想要的自己，而是把孩子培养成了你最想要的他。

爱，是圆的！当生命终止的时候，你所有赋予这个世界的爱都会随着这个圆回到你的身边。

你用心选择了你的爱侣，意味着同时也选择了他的父母。如果你选择了他（她）做伴侣，那就一定要用足够的耐心，无私地去对他（她）的父母好。因为，当父母含着泪把他（她）交给了你时，也就等于把他们生命里最重要的东西交给了你。所以，无论对方父母是否过于苛责，你都必须学会去感谢为你养育了一个陪伴自己一生的人。

从小时候父母教你开始说话起，你一直都在讲真话。长大后，有一天因你讲真话而遭批评时，你就开始学会了说假话。同时，还为自己说假话找了一个名字，叫做“善意的谎言”。

夫妻如镜，彼此相照。两人生活久了，每一个细微的变化心里都有感应。因此在照镜子时，傻比聪明更智慧。

生儿育女不仅是为了传宗接代、养儿防老，而是为了亲历一个生命的成长的过程，用无私的爱来传承生命的奇迹。

爱一个人并不一定天天在一起，也不是天天都说“我爱你”，而是在彼此的心里始终支持着对方。

失去的爱情曾经属于你，离开是因为你曾经的忽略。留下的爱情或许属于你，驻足是因为你用心地在乎。爱，只要在你身边，皆因彼此呼应疼惜，水乳交融；爱，如果离你而去，皆为一方不曾珍惜，渐行渐远。

当你把你的习惯和你的渴求不顾一切地用爱的名义强加给他人时，这份爱已经失去原本的美丽而成为一种令人窒息的压力。

你一定不会相信，他人的感觉和你自己的感觉已经相去甚远，当你陶醉于自我实现的良好感受之中时，你曾经的挚友们已渐行渐远。因为你不会看到并接受自己的弱点，而且还会用很多理由为自己证明辩解。

真正爱你的人不会宣扬你的隐私，而是为你守口如瓶，并真正站在你身边给你力量和温暖。

婚姻是夫妻两个人之间的事情，任何第三方的介入和干预都是野蛮和不明智的。如果恰巧你周围有这样以关怀的名义越过婚姻疆界的人，他不是第三者就是好事者。请记住，最好的夫妻是互信且互爱的心意互通的人，“解决办法比问题多”同样适用于婚姻！

用心经营婚姻的人，婚姻一定会长久；把婚姻当儿戏的人，婚姻也会同他（她）

游戏一场。

父爱无边，爱子无形。母爱如水，润子无声。天地之始，父母之交，孕万物之灵，育人类文明，开创繁衍生息之道。故有我们立世之本，利他之德，感恩之心。所以，敬父爱母不在节日当天，而是每时每刻。

无论多么好的风筝都脱离不了牵系它的线，无论你有多大的成就，都离不开家人和父母的支持与关爱。谨记，高飞时注意安全，家人这根线还时时维系在你的身边。

彼此能到走一起需要共同努力，不要等到分手之后，才后悔当初没好好珍惜。记住，她需要的是懂她的人，而不是限制她的人。

与善友相交，日久而不闻其香，然身心都已被清香润泽。

如果彼此的心没有距离，世上无论多远的距离都不算远。

平时对待家人的态度，有人品最真实的一面。

若想相守一生，就必须学会相互扶持，相互尊重，相互信任，才能走到最后。

与其说是过节陪伴家人，不如说在过节时寻找心的回归。心在回归时，自己和家人之间的能量才能得以流通和守恒。

能陪伴你到最后的不一定是需要你为之做什么的人，但一定是无论何时都愿意倾听你的人。

最真挚的友谊不是锦上添花而是雪中送炭。

真爱不是花言巧语的讨好，而是无微不致的关心。

GREE

It is necessary to carry on the family's bloodline, but more importantly to inherit the family spirit you take pride in.

Never do anything illegal in the name of honoring your parents because parents would rather suffer themselves than receive their children's filial duty in this way.

Communication between humans is not on body level but on spiritual level. Hatred will estrange two hearts while love will bring them together.

Without permission, never give away the personal information of your friends to someone else whatever the reason is. If you do so, it just proves that you don't regard them as your true friends.

The confidence of a man comes from the encouragement of a woman and that of a woman comes from the appreciation from a man.

It is acceptable to make a joke in our fast-paced life. But it should be remembered that life can be relaxing while your behaviors should not be imprudent. Our manners can be relaxed and natural but never dissolute and frivolous. Especially when associating with the opposite gender, your frivolous behaviors will show disrespect to others.

It is known to all that parents are the best teachers of a kid. Actually, kids can be teachers of their parents because kids are just like a mirror of their parents - the strengths and weaknesses of the parents can be completely reflected through their children.

If you love someone, just tell her or him. Never love someone in the name of friendship. But if you don't love someone, you'd better refuse him or her in the name of friendship to avoid hurting them.

Appreciating someone doesn't require a reason. People in your life are all passersby. Some of them you encounter and then forget; some of them you may give a glance but only to appreciate their beauty.

Women need care and love but don't think about this only during festivals.

Kinship, friendship as well as love are all destined. Therefore, don't be sad for estrangement and abandonment. It is unwise to regret and be addicted to the past affection which will never come back.

The best way to show gratitude to parents is not just give them money and material things but do things which can make them happy and proud of you. And you shall never make them ashamed.

You should love yourself before loving him or her as loving yourself is not selfishness but the basis of the principles for love.

When enjoying the happy festival and the happiness of family time, don't forget there are a lot of people who gave up the opportunity to be together with their family and stay at their jobs for the whole nation and for others' happiness and safety.

When you are extremely addicted to someone or something, you will only feel a transient joy and at last it always turns out that bitterness is much more than joys. Perhaps only those who have experienced it can have deep understandings about the bitterness of love.

Those who get married only for fame or fortune will swallow their pain at last.

Fellowship of men and women is like giving oneself some water to relieve his or her thirst, in which the moral bottom line must be followed because an instant love is like the snow falling from the sky, which will just melt in warmth.

Those trapped by affection and attracted by things are too many to name from the past to today. If you can escape from the traps of affection and things, acquire new enlightenment from past things, and find new wisdom from past emotions, you will be free and find your real self.

Not feeling loved doesn't mean there is no love around you. It is likely that the one who is accompanying you has his or her own way to express love.

That you are hurt doesn't mean others hurt you intentionally. It is perhaps because you are a little too sensitive.

What's the definition of a good friend? A good friend is someone who gets along with you without any personal agenda, who will help you out when you are in trouble, and who will never flatter you when you become rich. No matter where you are and whether you have power or high social status, a good friend will always send good wishes to you during Spring Festival and other holidays.

If breaking up is unavoidable, then you should adjust your own mood. Leave the memory in an unreachable deep corner of your heart, and never mention it again.

If there is no passion between a couple, please don't forget the feelings between each other. When deciding to let it go, you should recall the reason why you decided to be with him or her originally.

The one who truly loves you will never leave you in your most difficult times.

Arguments between couples or lovers are inevitable, but if they end up with a fight or violence, it will cause pain for each other. Therefore, no matter how angry you are, never resolve to violence.

In a marriage, there is no better way to kill a relationship than to hold resentments after a quarrel.

Those who are busy with making money and seeking gains while refusing to help others are actually pitiful because they have no ties of friendship even though they work hard all their lives.

There is a kind of love, which isn't based on benefits, ties of friendship or blood relations. Instead, it is one beyond the mundane relationship. The man who loves others as much as loving himself is offering true love.

The friendship based on cakes and ale is not the true one. Friendship can blossom only with a completely sincere heart and after being watered by love, fertilized by time and weeded by wisdom.

Whether he or she loves you or not, you have only one chance to encounter him or her this lifetime. If not cherishing the present moment when you are together, you will never see each other again regardless of your feelings about him or her.

Please don't always mention what you have done for the country, the people or the family, relatives or friends. Also don't show off your advantages or compare your contributions to others'. This is because what you have done prepares your own fortune and happiness while being overly proud is draining the fortune you have been working for.

It is easy to fall in love but difficult to get along. Due to different environments and values, everyone has his or her own feelings when stepping into a relationship, in which either happiness or bitterness is only clearly known by himself or herself.

When feeling tired during your love journey, don't change your initial mind. Calm down and ask yourself whether you love the blooming snow lotus on a mountain summit or the lunar plum at hand (whether you love what you want or what you have).

People seek love to step into marriage, but those in marriage have great difficulties finding the ideal love.

A woman who is not afraid of tiredness and wants to fill her life with work so that she wouldn't be hurt because of helplessness.

Lonely love may be particularly poignant and touching, but it is better to have someone who understands you and accompanies you in your need.

Don't be sad when saying goodbye because the short separation prepares you for the next meeting; don't be excited at meeting someone because today's meeting may be the last.

Everyone in your life is destined to be there. No matter whether it is a favorable or unfavorable affinity, just accept it with your heart. It can be a true destiny after your acceptance; otherwise, the same affinity will appear around you again some other day.

There is no way to stop a woman's gradual aging. Therefore, when appreciating a young beauty, don't forget to accept the mature beauty appearing in the aging process.

Making a good friend can lead to wealth or nobility while making a bad friend will cause bitterness or failure.

Friends can benefit each other but shouldn't make use of each other. Those who are used to taking advantage of their friends will never acquire true friends.

To show the romantic love between men and women is not to embrace or kiss each other in public. Instead, we should always think about creating a moving and romantic atmosphere for each other's spirit or daily life.

Regardless how high your artistic attainments are, never compare the value of works to friendship because as long as you attach more importance to the value of your works than to friendship, you will be utterly isolated in a short time.

Don't misunderstand that love between women and men must be accompanied with sex. This idea is just an excuse for those in need and desire for sex. When truly loving the other, you won't ask for an absolute sexual relationship, and you will put yourself in his or her position to protect his or her reputation according to moral standards.

It is our own loyalty and sense of responsibility rather than others that decides the happiness in marriage. All those who think their marriages are disasters contribute less while wanting more. They are always thinking about whether their gains are as much as they pay. What's more, they are suspicious of their companions' sincerity.

Neither a woman as beautiful as an angel but without a kind heart nor a handsome man without a sense of responsibility and commitment will be the right companion in your life.

True love can go beyond the length of life, the width of heart and the depth of soul. Therefore, just focus on the intrinsic quality rather than the external form or disguise.

Affections vary due to depth and the time they can be kept for. Extreme splendor is easy to burst into flames, after which all will turn into ashes. If you want to keep positive emotions, you should be devoted to them, and adjust wisely.

Only those who respect and are good to their parents will make true friends. Otherwise, the friends they make are often not the kind ones.

However great a man is, he has a weak point; however gentle a woman is, she has a strong side. Therefore, we need to be tolerant of men's weakness and understanding of the mightiness of women.

Couples have four kinds of fate between them, namely, showing gratitude, avenging a grievance, collecting debt and paying debt. Whatever the fate is, just learn to cherish the fate you possess. This is because a relationship between any couple will come to an end even though you love each other. When it comes to the end of life, you will never see each other.

It seems that there is someone not close to you, but when you get into trouble, he will never stand by. But when you get out of the trouble and want to thank him, you will find that he has left quietly. Don't use money to thank this kind of person because he has no desire for your money. Instead, what he hopes is that you can help

those in need around you and deliver love with them together.

The strong outside advice may not make a man understand true love. The easier one to imitate is to love others selflessly in the same way our parents love us. With frequent attempts and efforts, our gains will be not only the rich love but also the improvement of our ability to love.

There is a saying that "relatives vary from the close to distant and friendship varies from deep to shallow." This saying is widely

used but not very reasonable. If everything begins with sincerity and no discrimination, treating others equally will lead to sincere emotional gains in the end.

When asking your friends to help you, you should think carefully before you act. If you can deal with the problem by yourself, then don't bother others. If it is difficult for your friend to help you, then don't expect they will be able to succeed in helping you.

If you miss a bus, you can wait for another one. But if you miss someone, you might miss this person for your whole life. Therefore, when meeting someone who is good to you, just cherish them because once lost, they will never come back.

A broken relationship is like a kite without string, which you can just let go. Rather than stick to the sweet memories of the past and not let go, letting it go is also a relief to yourself. If you entangle yourself in an unhappy love relationship, you will only get hurt and feel sorrowful.

Blame yourself like you blame others and forgive others like you forgive yourself. Thus, the hard ice of a misunderstanding will melt gradually; the kinship, friendship and love relationship will also recover. When opening a window for others, you are also letting yourself watch the golden sunshine.

It is normal to have an admiration and affection for someone, but do not see that as the romantic type of love. The tempting heart is as delightful as a sapphire, which makes you feel dazzled. But true love is like sunshine: it feels ordinary as days grow; but once you lose it, you will find your whole world falls into darkness.

Bosom friends are those who know each other well and have a close emotional tie. They have mutual respect, appreciation and tolerance. When you have trusted much of your feelings and emotions to someone, are you not actually seeking another you in life?

It is an affinity to meet someone, which you must cherish. But cherishment is not just your own business. If your passion is met with indifference, don't be sad, because not everyone you know likes your personality and style. Those becoming your friends will at least have the same ideals and follow the same path with you.

The strongest love is to respect the beginning and be cautious of the end, which will probably and luckily be a moving masterpiece.

Those who regard you as a friend will never delete you from their contacts and all those refusing you to see their updates in

WeChat Moments won't treat you as a friend.

If there are ten children in a family, in which nine have no incomes while only one is working hard, the one will have to work even harder to support the whole family. What will happen if this phenomenon expands to the whole society?

The pure love is that you still want to be with your partner after all the freshness, passion and romantic feelings are taken away.

Love of high quality is that you love someone dearly and think for him or her for a lifetime.

Love is a fantastic consensual feeling that makes people willing to connect with others.

Children are reflecting mirrors of their parents and the defaults they show are all worth parents' self-reflection. When there are problems with the children, stop blaming the problems on the children, the schools, the teachers, or society etc. Instead, find the answer from the parents themselves. When children get into problems, parents should pay attention to the children's feelings and listen to them rather than just criticize them with the so-called forever correct opinions.

Love is a catalyst for sweetness promised by strangers on the same journey.

True love is a mutual discovery and acceptance both in sense and sensibility. It is a happy choice in life toward the future.

Only attentive appreciation of beautiful scenes can lead to the understanding of beauty. Beautiful women, likewise, require careful love, and thus you can acquire one's heart.

Love can encase the bitterness and sorrow and make every day in love shine!

The true friendship is that friends are still good to you, even though you have no value any more to them.

When you take a wife, if you only judge her by appearance instead of her virtue, you will regret it for your whole life. So, don't set fire to your house to keep yourself warm.

Giving so much over to you and not daring to look around, I prefer being hurt by the love finally to missing you and leaving you forever.

Is there any space for a clear sky in your heart? Even though you will never encounter the one and wait for a deep love alone, your loneliness of waiting is still showing the power of love!

Marriages or love of celebrities and public figures are not suitable as the perfect reference for yours and have no value to follow. Every partner in a marriage should find the most suitable place in a normal marriage life to compose a cadenza of their family

life. But still there are many people who don't know the happy marriage comes from persistence and cherishment instead of the frequent changes of the sheet music.

To debate with a critical friend will enable you to distinguish truth from falsities; to make a dialogue with your own heart will show a true you!

The so-called soulmate refers to the travelling companion who explores the deep truths in life, who appreciates your uniqueness and rebellion, and who pampers you in weakness and hardship. Also, a soul mate experiences and feels all the joys and sorrows with you together. He or she will stand by you and protect you in any situation. A soul mate is just like another self in the real world, which is really a destiny's favor!

The one loving you perhaps doesn't truly understand you. But if the one who understands you also loves you, then that love will be closer to the soul.

We usually tend to make habit-based mistakes such as easy to fall in love while hard to stay in love. We originally mean to show mutual respect, appreciation and tolerance, but end up just relieving our negative feelings to the one we love and frequently finding fault and hurting each other with a lousy choice of words. After all of this, you just keep regretting. This kind of paradox between the original intention and the behavior afterwards is caused by our extreme certainty but at the same time extreme uncertainty about love.

I'd like to give you the most appropriate amount of love, no more no less. The two of us just accompany each other quietly. I don't expect your commitment for hundreds of years, and I am willing to be with you every day!

Marriage connected by "love" and "affection" is a fusion of two hearts filled with sincerity and bravery; it is a fusion of two devoted emotions filled with joy and happiness. The success of such a combination of "love" and "affection" is because of the willingness to shoulder the responsibilities rising from love and affection.

A rose will not lose its beauty because of its thorns; a woman will not be unsuited for marriage because of her adamance and stubbornness. As long as you love her, just try to appreciate and accept the thorns in her.

When leaving a place, you cannot take the beautiful scene with you; after missing someone, everything has moved on from you. Only by experiencing a lot will you look at it clearly that some losing is more dependable than possessing.

Enjoy the simple joys in daily life alone; enjoy every moment in life alone. Don't be bothered by the coming and leaving of fate and just accept all the joys and sorrows it brings.

I have been seeking that main character in my story not until I realized my story would not even begin until you come into my life.

There are three stages in a relationship progressing to marriage: the honey stage of courting, in which everything of the lover is appreciated even all shortcomings; the confrontation stage, in which all defaults are shown and merits are neglected,

leading to a battle for control and bitterness; the mature stage, in which the proper way to get along with each other is acquired after a long process of painful adjustments and self-growth. At last, a home for love is finally established.

Only when you are at your low point will you understand the value of friendship. If you have never experienced solitude, how can you find out who is your true friend and who is the one offering you deep emotions and warmth?

There are some words I always wanted to say to you but I never did. Today, I take my courage to tell you that encountering you is a beautiful surprise and I will cherish you.

Love will never be missed, for it has an eternal guarantee period. Missing love doesn't mean that it is a mistake, or it has passed by. Instead, it means that this love doesn't deserve to be called love or it doesn't belong to you.

Men are like mountains while women water. They are not deadly enemies and they should keep a relationship that compliments each other. If you are as magnificent as mountains, she will be bright as water. If she is as soft as water and as warm as jade, then you can be tolerant like seas and mountains. This state of being closely related and mutually dependent is the best stage.

Men are shadows of women. How you shine light on them will determine what the shadows look like; women are mirrors of men. How you treat them will reflect thoroughly in the mirror.

If people's marriages originate from love rather than temptation of vanity and material things, then the nice wishes of marriages are to keep the purity and warmth of love. An ideal marriage is accompanied by love from the beginning to the end without temptations to depart as days grow long. Love is decided by two persons, so face the plain life with trials and hardships hand-in-hand and never forget the passion and care in the original love while being busy with transient mundane. Getting along with the heart is the secret of keeping marriage sweet and happy. So did you make an effort wholeheartedly today?

The real difference between liking someone and loving someone is that the former means much possession and acquisition while the latter tends to give and offer more. Just remember that love can only be gained with a true heart!

Is there a clear line between friendship and love? And can these two relationships be interchangeable? Will a friendship change into touching love as friendship deepens? Will love return to friendship if affection disappears? Actually, a formula for conversion doesn't exist between the two; however, there is indeedly something in common between the two: the requirement of cherishing each other. I'd like to offer you a piece of advice: don't be greedy or stupid;

otherwise you will lose both love and friendship, and the two of you will become strangers at last.

How long will the longest marriage last? Perhaps the answer is less than one hundred years. If you profligate and show no respect, it will come to an end more quickly. When a marriage becomes irreversible, you will have no way to fix it but sigh over the loss.

Do cherish the present day because it is likely that we will never meet each other again tomorrow.

Love at first sight is an affectionate spark. Whether or not the spark can turn into the fire of love depends on fate and sincerity.

When you want to complain, there is someone to understand your feelings. When saying something warm to the loving and loved one, you will feel togetherness even if there is a long distance between the two of you!

The smack of missing has two forms: one is sweet; one is bitter.

Marriage is neither the tomb for love nor the silver bullet. Therefore, love isn't supposed to be changed by marriage but expected to cure marriage.

Marriage shows mutual appreciation and love while divorce shows no tolerance even when there is still love.

Women's beauty is various and numerous, but the most touching one is kindness, with which a woman, like a tranquil lake, loves life and stays in love quietly.

The filial duties and gratitude are more than cultural symbols

inherited from the ancestors. Instead, they are life habits closely related to the work and life of everyone. When practiced and passed on, those filial duties will develop into the Dao of filial piety because of the accumulation of gratitude.

Those praising you every day may not be the ones loving you, and they will be the first ones to leave you if you cannot meet their needs. Those pointing out your mistakes occasionally may not be the ones not loving you, and they will be the first ones to help you when you get into trouble.

The beauty of life lies in sticking with something rather than competing for something. Marriage is just like that!

The many things you ask of your children will not shape them into who they want to be. On the contrary, you make them who you want them to be.

Love is a circle. When life comes to an end, all the love you have given to the world will come back to you again.

You choose your partner with your heart, which means you have also chosen his or her parents at the same time. Since you have chosen your partner, please be nice to his or her parents. When your partner was handed to you by the parents with tears, it means that they gave you what is most important in their lives. Therefore, regardless of how critical they are of you, you have to learn to thank them for bringing up the one who is to accompany you in your life.

You have been telling the truth since you were taught to speak by your parents. Growing up, when you are criticized for telling the truth one day, you learn to tell a lie. At the same time, you name the lie a "white lie".

A husband and a wife are mirrors of each other; they reflect

each other mutually. After living together for a long time, you will find even slight changes will touch your hearts. Therefore, it is much wiser to be silly rather than clever when looking in the mirror.

Having children is not only to carry on the family line and to support yourselves in old age, but also to experience the process of growing life and to pass the miracle of life with selfless love.

It is unnecessary to be together every day to show you love someone or keep saying "I love you" every day. Instead, you should support each other in your hearts, always.

The lost love used to belong to you; you lost it because of neglect. The love remaining may belong to you; you still have it because of your sincere care. Love will be with you if you cherish each other and get along with each other; love will abandon you if you don't cherish each other and drift apart.

When you impose your habits and desires on others recklessly in the name of love, your love has lost the original beauty and turned into a painful pressure.

You may never believe that other's feelings and your own feelings are greatly different. When you are indulged and lost in your achievements, your close friends may have drifted away from you because you not only cannot realize your weaknesses but also use many excuses to justify yourself.

The one who truly loves you will never expose your privacy; instead, he or she will keep silent and stand by you to offer you strength and warmth.

Marriage is a matter between the husband and the wife. Any interference from a third party is uncivilized and unwise. If there is someone who breaks the bond of marriage in the name of caring, this

someone is either an adulterer or a busy body. Please remember that the best couples are those who believe in and understand each other. The saying that "there are more solutions than there are problems" is suitable for marriage.

Those who manage marriage with heart will have a long-lasting marriage while those who regard marriage as a game will be tricked by marriage in return.

A father's love is without limit, doled out to the children in countless ways; a mother's love is like water, nurturing the children quietly. Since the beginning of heaven and earth, the parents gave birth to all souls, cultivated human civilization, and created the way for humans to multiply and prosper. Our foundations for life, altruism, and gratitude are thus born. Therefore, showing respect and love for parents should not be on the day of a festival, but rather at every moment.

The best kite does not break away from its tether; the most accomplished person cannot be without the support and love from family and parents. Remember to be safe when flying high and keep this family tether with you always.

Being together this time life requires mutual efforts. Do not wait until after the break-up to regret not cherishing then. Remember what she needs is someone who understands her, not someone who restricts her.

Having a good friend, although you may not notice the friend's merits after some time, your body and soul have been permeated with their kind characters and traits.

If there is no distance between two hearts, no distance in the world is far.

The attitude toward family members day in and day out is the truest of one's characters.

To live "till death do us part", we must learn to support, respect and trust each other. Only then can we travel to the end together.

Rather than saying it is spending time with family during holidays, it is best to think it is finding the return of the heart during the holidays. Only when the mind returns can the energy between oneself and family members circulate and remain constant.

The one who can accompany you to the end is not necessarily someone who needs you to do anything for them, but someone who is willing to listen to you any time.

The most sincere friendship is not adding flowers to the brocade to improve what is already good but sending charcoal during a snow to provide timely help.

True love is not using sweet words to ingratiate oneself, but caring for the loved one in every possible way.

第六章

艺苑诗情篇 / Art poetry

陽光

中国画的艺术特征在世界艺术长廊中是独一无二的，它集中体现了东方美学思想。其中，儒、释、道哲学思想是形成和孕育其艺术特征的精神家园。

为什么荷花常得画家青睐？荷花可以表示“本固枝荣”，多用于祝人世代绵延、家道昌盛。荷花的“荷”因与“和”同音，所以国画中常用来寓意“和睦”“和顺”。小幅的荷花小品适合挂卧室，是男女好合、夫妻恩爱的象征。荷有莲蓬，因莲蓬与花同时生长，故莲籽寓意“早生贵子”，莲蓬也象征多多生子。荷花出污泥不染，在东南亚是有的国家的国花，佛教是圣人仙座，圣洁之意，是圣花。还代表有根，世代绵延昌盛。

败笔是学习过程中的历练，不敢面对败笔难以进步。

从小在河边长大的孩子不学游泳也知水性，禀性如同莲花般的人不去拜师也自会画荷。

画的是精神，写的是人生。观的是笔墨，看的是灵魂。

由心而生的画远比为了画而画的作品更通透有灵性，带着目的去搞创作不及自在时那一笔水墨更超然物外。

无论日月星辰怎样轮转，内心深处那份对荷的欣赏和理解永远不变。正是这份洒脱才让笔下的荷栩栩如生，有春夏秋冬之变化，出污泥而不染的净雅。

画荷时非画荷，而是用笔墨尽染白纸人生，与笔墨纸砚对话，寻找笔墨知音，自由展现荷的精魂。

画画的最高境界不是形似，也非神似，而是介于两者之间，兼具且高于两者。

有一种美叫脱俗，唯有脱俗的美才是最接近自然的美。

月光之美是静静的阴柔之美，如果你烦恼积聚，则可静心于天地之间，让月光挥洒你的全身，化解你的烦躁与孤独。

你看树孤独，其实是你自己孤独。树不仅有四季相随，还有风雨雾雪雷电相伴。早上有鸟儿在枝头高歌，夜间还有小虫低吟相伴。你看树孤独吗？你不是树根本不懂树的乐趣。树自己的乐趣并不局限于这些陪伴，而是她能随风歌唱，她能春生、夏茂、秋落、冬藏，无论四季怎么更迭，六道如何轮回 ，一直在默默地享受你所谓的孤独。

月亮越明亮，古老的石头越静。不是因为石头爱慕月亮，而是因为石头想要把这无声的爱反射给所有需要光的众生。

The artistic characteristics of Chinese painting, which fully embody the aesthetics of Asia, are unique in the world art gallery. Confucianism, Buddhism and Taoism are the spiritual homes that form and nurture these artistic characteristics.

Why are lotus flowers often favored by painters? Lotus flowers represent the meaning of "solid roots and lustrous branches" and often are used to wish people and family to proper for generations. The Chinese character " 荷 " for lotus flower is a homophone to the character "和," which means "harmony" and "smooth." Thus, lotus flowers are also used in Chinese paintings to show such meaning of "harmony and smooth." A small lotus painting is suitable for hanging in the bedroom; it is a symbol of love between men and women, and the love between husband and wife.

Faulty strokes in painting is an experience in the learning process. It is difficult to make progress if one dares not face the faulty strokes.

Children growing up along the riverbank can tread water without taking swim lessons. People whose nature resembles that of a lotus flower can paint lotus without learning from a teacher.

What a painter paints is the spirit; what he presents is life. What a spectator sees is the ink and what he saw is the soul.

The paintings born from the heart are far more spiritual than the works painted for the purpose of painting. Creating with a purpose is less transcendent than painting at ease.

No matter how times flies and seasons change, the appreciation and understanding of lotus flowers remains unchanged. Because of this, the locus flowers, born under a paint brush, renders the seasonal changes and retains the purity and elegance.

When painting lotus flowers, it is not necessarily just painting lotus; rather, it is a process using brush and ink to paint life on paper; it is a dialogue with the brush, the link, and the paper to exhibit the spirit of the lotus flowers.

The highest state of painting is neither the resemblance of the appearance nor that of the spirit; rather it is something in between. It includes both resemblance but goes above both.

There exists a kind of beauty which is called refined. Only refined beauty is the beauty closest to nature.

The beauty of the moonlight is that of femininity. If your worries are built up, let the moonlight shine on you and resolve the agitation and loneliness as you ease your mind.

You may regard the tree as lonely, but in fact it is not the tree but yourself that is lonely. The trees are not only followed by the four seasons, but also accompanied by wind, rain, fog, snow, thunder and lightning. In the morning, birds sing in the branches; at night worms hum quietly. Do you think the trees are lonely? You are not a tree and how can you know the joy of a tree? The delight of a tree is not limited to having all the companies, but its ability to sing with the wind, grow in the spring, prosper in the summer, wither in the fall and reserve energy in the winter. No matter how the seasons change and how the six realms transmigrate, the trees silently enjoy the "loneliness" you have deemed.

The brighter the moonlight, the more still the age-old stone. It is not because the stone loves the moonlight; rather, the stone wants to reflect and give this silent love to those who need the light.

■ 后 记

多年前，一位新闻界的老前辈说，把一件小事写成长篇大论不足为奇，把复杂的事用寥寥数语写出来才是真本事。为了练就老前辈说的“真本事”，我试着从写小的感言开始练笔，坚持每天早晚各写一句。这些感言全是源于记者的职业敏感，从身边的人和事的经验积累中提炼出来的。

最初只是发给身边的亲朋好友分享，后来在大家的鼓励下才萌生了把它们整理成册、印刷出版的想法。

从开始整理《陽光心语》准备出版至今，得到了社会各界好友的鼎力相助。对于这些一直以来给予支持和帮助的爱心人士，陽光的肺腑之言无以言表。衷心感谢整理、校对书稿的资深出版人李勇、谢宇，资深媒体人陈达，好友庄丽老师，上海师范大学石立善教授（已故）；为陽光画像的漫画家赵和平；为书名题字的李一、郭宝庆等著名书法家；为图书配图的何家英、卢禹舜、刘万鸣、陈孟昕、穆家善、杨华山、刘立军、李宏禹、心田等著名书画家；在书稿翻译校对方面给予友情帮助的刘艳教授、王民卉教授、罗兰老师、汪宁大夫、孙瀚晓；在经济上或其他出版事务中给予无私援助的白丽媛、白怡嘉、鲍红艳、曹国庆、曹文琦、曹晓伟、陈愈萱、陈子瑜、戴婧媛、冯淑霞、高山、耿春华、宫乃林、关长虹、关凯红、黄波、黄楠、井红旗、郎彬、郎莉、李君、李敏、李沐晨、李晓辉、李晓芸、李秀珍、李旭、李禹辉、李梓正、梁康、林文苹、刘卫兵、刘岩、刘增爱、路占芳、吕东梅、吕清民、马世春、马卫、潘益新、庞淑霞、朴金子、秦楠、邱淦清、莎莎、商春杰、尚淑文、孙秀明、陶星迪、田健弘、田钰诚、王丽、王宁宁、王士群、王艳霞、王莹、韦瑞敏、武军、夏传磊、谢宇、徐云鹏、许子潍、杨斌、杨佳政、杨璐、杨树生、杨轶伦、叶瑞君、余莲荣、于梦迪、战博、张传疆、张凤、张宏萍、张泓杨、张普敬、张小杰、张晓荣、张燕辉、张彦杰、张益钧、赵洪英、赵时展、赵艳等好友。还有诸多师友的善行功绩，不能一一列出，也在此表示衷心的感谢。因为有诸位的大力支持，这本小册子才能顺利付梓。

还要向自己深爱着的父母、妻儿这几年来给予的大力支持表示感谢。同时也向恩师蒋铎、王莒生、王麟鹏、毛克臣、龚宇以及社会各界爱心人士给予的支持与帮助表示诚挚的谢意。感恩诸位的大爱之心，让这本“爱心之语”能和大家见面。

在这本小册子面世的背后，有着雷波“爱心橙”团队和更多爱心人士对公益事业的希望和汗水。在此，我再次对他们给予的无私帮助深表谢意。希望这些大爱能再次循环到他们身边，让整个世界因为你我他的大爱之心变得更加温暖。

陽光於北京厚德居

戊戌年癸亥月庚戌日

Years ago, an elder respected person in media said, "It is not at all surprising to write a long speech about a trivial matter; it is a true skill, however, to write about complicated things in a few words."To practice what this senior person referred to as "true skill," I tried to start writing short reflections, which turned into a habit of writing one sentence each day both in the morning and in the evening. These reflections originated in the sensitivity developed by my journalism profession and drew material from both the experience of the people and the events around me.

At first, I only shared my reflections with friends and family. Later on, encouraged by my friends and family, I had the idea of putting the writing together for publication.

From compiling material for "Words of Sunshine" to preparing for its publication, I have received countless help from good friends from all walks of life. To those caring people who have been supporting and helping me all this time, heart-felt words cannot express my gratitude.I would like to express my heartfelt thanks to the senior publishers Mr. Li Yong and Mr. Xie Yu, the senior correspondent Mr.Chen Da, my good friend Zhuang Li, and the late professor Shi Lishan from Shanghai Normal University, for their help and efforts in collating and proofreading the manuscript; cartoonist Zhao Heping, who did the portrait of Yang Guang in the book; Li Yi, Guo Baoqing and other famous calligraphers, who did the inscription for the book; He Jiaying, Lu Yushun, Liu Wanming,

Chen Mengxin, Mu Jiashan,Yang Huashan,Liu Lijun, Li Hongyu, Xin Tian and other famous painters, who did the illustration; Professor Liu Yan and Wang Minhui and Luo Lan, Doctor Wang Ning,Sun Hanxiao who offered friendly help translating the book into English and proof-reaing; BaiLiyuan, BaiYijia, Bao Hongyan, Cao Guoqing , Cao Wenqi, Cao Xiaowei, Chen Yuxuan, Chen Ziyu, Dai Jingyuan, Feng Shuxia, Gao Shan, Geng Chunhua, Gong Nailin, Guan Changhong, Guan Kaihong, Huang Bo, Huang Nan, Jing Hongqi, Lang Bin, LangLi, Li Jun, Li Min, Li Muchen, Li Xiaohui, Li Xiaoyun, Li Xiuzhen, Li Xu, Li Yuhui, Li Zizheng, Liang Kang, Lin Wenping, Liu Weibing, Liu Yan, Liu Zengai, Lu Zhanfang, Lv Dongmei, Lv Qingmin, Ma Shichun, Ma Wei, Pan Yixin, Pang Shuxia, Piao Jinzi, Qin Nan, Qiu Ganqing, Sha Sha, Shang Chunjie, Shang Shuwen, Sun Xiuming, Tao Xingdi, Tian Jianhong, Tian Yucheng, Wang Li, Wang Ningning, Wang Shiqun, Wang Yanxia, Wang Ying, Wei Ruimin, Wu Jun, Xia Chuanlei, Xie Yu, Xu Yunpeng, Xu Ziwei, Yang Bin, Yang Jiazheng, Yang Lu, Yang Shusheng, Yang Yilun, Ye Ruijun, Yu Lianyong, Yu Mengdi, Zhan Bo, Zhang Chuanjiang, Zhang Feng, Zhang Hongping, Zhang Hongyang, Zhang Pujing, Zhang Xiaojie, Zhang Xiaorong, Zhang Yanhui, Zhang Yanjie, Zhang Yijun, Zhao Hongying, Zhao Shizhan,

Zhao Yan and other friends who those that have given unselfish help in financial support or other publishing matters. There are many other people who offered valuable help and I regret not being able to list everyone here. I express my heartfelt thanks to all of them. It is only with their support can this book successfully go into publication.

I wanted to thank my beloved parents, my wife and children for their support in the past few years. My thanks also go to my teachers Jiang Duo, Wang Jusheng, Wang Linpeng, Mao Kechen, Gong Yu and many loving people from all walks of life for their support. Because of their loving hearts, this book "Words of Sunshine" can be read by many.

Behind the publication of this book, there stands Lei Bo's "Loving Orange" team and many other loving people who devoted their time and effort to public and community service. Once again, I give my sincere appreciation to their selfless devotions. I hope this love will circle back to them; I wish the world a warmer and more loving place because of the loving hearts from us all.

By Yang Guang at Beijing Houdeju

Gengxu Day, Kuihai Month, Wushu Year

風起雲湧